*"Is this the m_____
to the happeni___ _____*

Elanna covered her mouth and swallowed a startled outcry. She whirled so fast at the voice that she lost her balance and would have landed in the bush had it not been for the strong arms that saved her from a fall. With both feet planted on solid ground again, she turned to look up at the interloper. Her heart skipped a beat.

Madison Scott stared down at her with an amused grin on his face. "Or perhaps to gain further information you also play upon the sympathies of innocent soldiers passing through town."

"Major Scott!" At his silent admonition and nod of his head toward the open window, Elanna lowered her voice. "I thought you had returned home to Boston."

AMBER MILLER is a freelance Web designer and author whose articles and short stories have appeared in local, national, and international publications. Her writing career began as a columnist for her high school and college newspapers. Her first publication in a book appeared in the form of nine contributions (as a single!) to *101 Ways to Romance Your Marriage* by Debra White Smith. She is a member of American Christian Fiction Writers and Historical Romance Writers. Some of her hobbies include traveling, music, movies, and interacting with other writers. At age three, she learned to read and hasn't put down books since. Recently married, she lives with her husband and fellow writer, Stuart, in beautiful Colorado Springs. Visit her Web site to learn more or to contact her: www.ambermiller.com.

Books by Amber Miller

HEARTSONG PRESENTS
HP784—Promises, Promises

Quills and Promises

Amber Miller

Heartsong Presents

Thank you to my husband, Stuart, and my family—Dad, Mom, Brett, Brad, and Steve, plus my newly extended family—for so much more than words here can express. To Linda Windsor, without your mentorship, this series wouldn't be a reality. Big thanks go out to everyone in ACFW, and to Jim and Tracie Peterson, who took a chance on me. And to all of my friends, who are far too numerous to name. Finally, thanks goes to God for giving me this gift of words. All glory and honor go to Him for the realization of this dream.

A note from the Author:
I love to hear from my readers! You may correspond with me by writing:

Amber Miller
Author Relations
PO Box 721
Uhrichsville, OH 44683

ISBN 978-1-60260-049-2

QUILLS AND PROMISES

All scripture quotations are taken from the King James Version of the Bible.

All of the characters and events in this book are fictitious. Any resemblance to actual persons, living or dead, or to actual events is purely coincidental.

Our mission is to publish and distribute inspirational products offering exceptional value and biblical encouragement to the masses.

PRINTED IN THE U.S.A.

one

"Chelcy!" Fifteen-year-old Elanna Hanssen waved at her best friend and crossed the cobblestone street toward the town green, lifting her petticoats to avoid the mud from the recent rains.

"Oh, Elanna, I am so happy to see you!" Chelcy Greyson embraced Elanna in a warm hug, then stepped back. Her eyes gleamed, and she looked ready to burst with whatever news she had to share.

"Tell me the latest before your stays snap."

Chelcy covered her mouth with her gloved hand and giggled. "Is it that obvious?"

Elanna gave Chelcy's arm a tug and led her toward the stone bench at the edge of the green. "When I saw you, I thought you had somehow managed to capture the sunlight and shine it through your eyes."

"How romantic!" Chelcy pressed her hands to her heart. "Is that from one of your poems or journals?"

"No, it is original and new as of today." Perhaps someday all of her writing would amount to more than ink blots on parchment paper. For now, however, her friend took center stage. Elanna pointed a finger at Chelcy. "No more delays. Tell me your news."

Chelcy clasped Elanna's hands in her own and bounced on

5

the stone bench. Elanna grinned at the enthusiastic display.

"I could hardly believe it when Mother and Father showed me the letter. It took so long to get here, and we only had three days to prepare for his arrival. We had not seen or heard from him in four years, and now he is here. It is so exciting. I do not know how I managed to remain calm this long. Mother had to remind me at least five times every day to relax and focus. Somehow, I completed my daily tasks and—"

"One moment," Elanna interrupted. "Slow down. You spoke so fast I only caught half of what you said. Now, what letter did you receive? And who sent it? Who is here?"

Chelcy touched two fingers to her lips and offered a sheepish grin. "Do forgive me. I told you how excited I was."

"Yes, that much I gathered. Will I ever get to hear who is visiting, or is that going to remain a surprise until I meet him?"

"My cousin," Chelcy announced in a rush. "His name is Madison Scott, and he is visiting from Massachusetts. There are reports that the war is spreading, and he wanted to spend some time with us before things get too bad."

A cousin? From the north? Elanna didn't know why that would be cause for such excitement, but Chelcy had enough exuberance for them both. This Madison must be held in high esteem with the Greysons since it appeared they had gone out of their way to prepare for his arrival. Elanna wanted to know more.

"So, your cousin is visiting. Is he somehow connected to the Boston Assembly or to some influential person?"

"He is not a councilman, no, but he does wield a certain amount of influence among the soldiers in his regiment."

A soldier. That explained some, at least. "He managed to get enough time away from his regiment to travel this far south? He must be more than a common soldier."

Chelcy nodded. "He is the eldest son of my uncle. After

spending several years serving in England in His Majesty's Royal Army and risking his life for his commanding officer during an attack by the French, he returned to Boston and has recently attained the appointment of major." She grinned. "You are going to love him."

"Are you singing my praises again, Chelcy? I must confess, the stories you tell make my accomplishments sound larger than life."

"Madison!" Chelcy jumped up from the bench and threw her arms around a rather dashing gentleman.

Elanna couldn't see quite enough of him to get a clear view of his face, but he did make a stylish figure in his uniform. He returned Chelcy's hug with equal fervor, then unwound her arms from his neck and stepped back to get a better look at her. When Chelcy turned again to face her, Elanna caught a full vision of her cousin. Dashing only dusted the surface of an accurate description.

"And who might this charming young lady be?"

Madison took a step toward her, removed his hat with a flourish, and bowed. Gallant and handsome. What a winning combination. A dangerous one, too. He was already leagues ahead of most gentlemen Elanna knew.

"Madison Scott, milady. Might I have the pleasure of an introduction?"

"Oh, Madison, cease with your frivolous social graces. This is Elanna Hanssen, my best friend."

The glint in his eyes accompanied a beguiling grin. "On the contrary, my dear cousin." His attention never wavered from Elanna's face. "One must always adhere to the social customs in order to guarantee a good first impression." He reached for one of Elanna's hands and raised it to his lips. "Would you not agree, Miss Hanssen?"

Elanna could barely remember her name, let alone come

up with an appropriate response to his query. By the gleam in his eyes, he certainly knew the effect he had on her. That only made a reply much more difficult. But she'd never backed down from a challenge before, and she didn't intend to start now. With all the grace she could muster, she withdrew her hand from his grasp. Snapping her fan in front of her with several brisk strokes, she took the needed moment to compose herself.

"I would say, Major Scott, that your observation is correct. Regardless of the circumstances, when in mixed company, one must always adhere to the social rules that govern polite society."

Chelcy released a dramatic groan. "Oh, Elanna! Not you, too."

Madison regarded Elanna with undisguised admiration. It was evident that his boldness wasn't met with indifference often; rather, he no doubt enjoyed great success with the ladies. Elanna wondered just how many ladies graced the soldier's life.

"And I gather that your family has raised you according to those same customs."

"Indeed. After all, Papa is a member of the assembly, and Mama is quite influential with the wives of the assembly members."

Elanna could count at least four times in the past month when the assembly wives had been invited to their home for tea. Something big loomed just beyond the horizon. She could feel it.

"It appears New Castle benefits greatly from the contributions of your family. From what my dear cousin tells me, it will not be long before these counties break off to become a colony in their own right."

Chelcy swatted Madison with her fan. "So you *did* read my letters."

Madison feigned insult and slapped his hat to his chest.

"But of course. Do you doubt my interest in local politics? You reside in a town that is situated close enough to Philadelphia to be a significant source of information."

Finally! A topic of interest to Elanna. Despite her mother's objections, Papa kept her informed about significant news from his meetings. Although not privy to everything, she learned enough to stay up to date.

She tried hard to contain her excitement. "From what Papa has told us at home, many members of the assembly wish to separate these counties from Pennsylvania so we can fully govern ourselves without their interference."

"And where is home, Miss Hanssen?"

"My family owns a farm a few miles southwest of town along the Christina River."

"Perhaps I shall be able to call upon you there someday."

Elanna dipped her head and brought her fan once more to shield her face. "Perhaps, Major Scott." The sooner, the better, for she was developing a great desire to enjoy his captivating presence and quick wit for more than these few moments.

It had been several months since a gentleman had turned her head. Her twin brother, Edric, teased her often about spending all of her time with pen and paper. But that was how she best expressed herself. God had gifted her with the ability to communicate using the written word, and she refused to waste that talent by ignoring it. Wouldn't Edric be surprised that she had met someone despite that solitary activity?

"Very well," Chelcy announced and stepped between them, "if you two insist upon this formal address, I believe I will return home and leave you both here to determine who will win the social skirmish."

Her friend's declaration dissipated the cloud that had fogged Elanna's mind since Madison had joined their conversation. Had she just been openly coy? Mama would lapse into vapors if she had witnessed such brazen behavior. She'd do well to rein in her actions and her tongue or else risk consequences far worse than her private guilt.

Chelcy touched Elanna's elbow and drew her out of her musings. "Will you be attending the town meeting with your father next week?"

Oh, the meeting! She'd almost forgotten. "Yes, of course. With Edric learning what's necessary to take his position come his eighteenth birthday, I would sooner miss my own birthday party than the opening of the assembly."

Her dramatic expression elicited a giggle from Chelcy and a chuckle from Madison.

"As always, delivered with flair and pomp." Chelcy smiled. "Is it any wonder why I find you a pure delight?"

Elanna placed a hand on her chest and raised her chin just a bit. "Just think how utterly dull your life would be without me in it."

"Perish the thought. I refuse to even think of such misery."

Madison raised one eyebrow. "And you accuse both Miss Hanssen and me of frivolous speech?"

A tinge of pink spotted Chelcy's cheeks. She snapped open her fan and hid behind the folds. "I do believe that is my cue to withdraw from this fine company." She motioned for Elanna to step aside with her. "Guard yourself, my friend," she cautioned in an undertone. "My dear cousin has a reputation with the ladies. I fear from your expression that you have already succumbed to his charm. Promise me you will keep your wits about you."

Elanna placed a hand on Chelcy's upper arm. "I assure you that my wits will remain firmly intact. Your cousin has done nothing more than behave as any gentleman would."

"I might consider him more of a rogue," Chelcy countered with a twinkle in her eyes.

"Be that as it may, you have no need to be bothered about me. I vow to remain in clear view of passersby. Edric and Papa and my three uncles would lock me in my room and teach your cousin a lesson with their fists should I do anything to cause tongues to wag."

A sigh escaped Chelcy's lips. Relief filled her expression. "Very well. I shall leave you alone together. . .as long as you promise to tell me all that transpired when you come to town again for the meeting next week."

Laughing, Elanna brushed cheeks with her friend. "I promise."

With that, Chelcy was gone. Flutters started in Elanna's stomach, and she placed a hand atop the affected area. Forcing herself to calm, she gave Madison her full attention, but he was the first to speak.

"Shall we?" He extended a hand toward the stone bench. She sat and tucked her skirts beneath her, laying her fan across her lap. A part of her knew she should probably start for home, but another part wanted to hear the news from this soldier. The latter part won.

ক

Madison regarded Elanna before he spoke. Something about the fair maiden captivated him. Perhaps it was her guileless nature or her winsome smile. Or it could be her engaging personality. Whatever it was, he felt compelled to enjoy her company for a little while longer.

"So, tell me more—"

"What is it like, living—"

They both laughed as their words tumbled over each other's.

Madison gestured, palm up, encouraging her to continue. "Please."

Elanna dipped her head, then returned her gaze to his. "I

would like to know more about your life as a soldier. I have overheard bits of conversation between Papa and several assembly members that have piqued my interest, but they tell me their affairs are not for a young lady's ears." A pout drew Madison's eyes to her lips. "I do not wish to pry, but I am fascinated by what little I do hear and long to know more."

He had best tread carefully, both in his errant thoughts and on this subject. Too much and he would face severe consequences when he returned to his regiment. Not enough and he would risk disappointing this very attractive young woman. Neither outcome held much appeal.

Madison shifted his attention back to her eyes and away from the more-engaging area of her lips.

"Tell me, first, how much you already know about the recent events in the north."

Elanna chewed on her bottom lip and gazed past his left shoulder. He took advantage of that moment to observe her unnoticed. Waves of wheat-colored hair were gathered with combs and fastened under a lappet cap. Eyes the deep gray of the wet sand along the cape near Boston hinted at wisdom beyond her years, yet her manner bespoke a youthful innocence that increasingly intrigued him. Knowledgeable about the facts but ignorant to the ways of the world, she couldn't possess more than ten and five years. If more, then the men of this town should be brought to question for not seeing the beauty before them.

The object of his scrutiny shifted her focus and caught him staring. A becoming blush stained her cheeks, and she tucked her chin to avert her gaze. Innocent indeed. A characteristic he found both refreshing and appealing. Unable to resist, Madison gave a feather-light touch to her cheek. The embarrassment changed to something warmer, but the doe-like innocence remained.

"Do forgive me. I must apologize for causing you discomfort. Please share with me what you know, and I will endeavor to supply the necessary facts to satisfy your curiosity."

His young companion brightened, and her enthusiasm once again took hold. "Over the past two years, Papa has often shared details of reports made to the assembly of the developments in the Ohio Valley and as far north as the St. Lawrence Valley. I understand the dispute over who owns the land beyond the mountains that has led to the war with the French, but I am unclear about how all of these recent events interconnect."

A sweet face paired with an intelligent mind. Such a combination Madison didn't often encounter in the women he knew.

"Basically, both the French and the English claim all the lands from the Alleghenies west to the Mississippi River. While the area along the St. Lawrence River has also been under dispute, the Ohio Valley has recently become the main focus of this conflict."

"Papa says the Ohio Territory is beautiful. From his description, I can almost see it—majestic rolling hills and valleys with glimmering crystal streams, how the rising and setting sun casts color and shadow across the landscape, and all of it stretching as far as the eye can see."

Not only intelligent, but a poet as well. He must learn more about this charming lady.

"Such a vivid imagination you possess," he said with a smile. "The problem is that the French claim they discovered this land, while we English claim it is ours by charter and by our alliance with the Iroquois."

Elanna pursed her lips. "If this land is as valuable as it is beautiful, any man would be foolish not to want it for his own." She tracked the progress of a butterfly alighting on a bed of flowers nearby. "This land here, west of the Delaware River and east of the Chesapeake, has a beauty all its own. I would gladly fight for it if someone challenged me to its ownership."

Madison straightened, frowning, astonished that he had found such a kindred spirit. She had no idea how much he had longed to find someone in whom he could confide; someone who wasn't a part of the regiment in which he served. Because he only associated with fellow soldiers and pompous assembly-men who found dalliances more agreeable than politics, Madison hadn't encountered anyone else who could hold a passable conversation with him. Never in his wildest imagination would he have expected to find such compatibility here in New Castle with a young lady.

Thankfully, Elanna's attention remained with the elusive butterfly. "That is the exact source of the dispute," he murmured. "If the French have their way, we English will be confined to this narrow space between the Atlantic and the crest of the Alleghenies. On the other hand, if the English have theirs, the French will be hemmed within a small portion north of the St. Lawrence."

The sudden flight of two blue jays overhead caught their attention. When the birds flew into a nearby tree, a squirrel chittered in protest. The birds flapped their wings, chirped a few times, and remained where they landed. Accepting defeat, the squirrel scampered down the trunk. Bounding over to another tree, he raced up to resume his previous activities. Elanna shared a smile with Madison at the little animal's antics before bringing their conversation back to the matter at hand.

"Why cannot England and France simply come to an accord on this issue?"

Madison sighed and shook his head. "In my opinion, greed

is the driving force that blinds them to any compromise."

Impulsively, Madison covered Elanna's hand with his, then quickly withdrew it, conscious of passersby. She didn't seem to notice, or at least showed no signs that she did. No need to cause her undue distress by making advances that would be misinterpreted by townsfolk who happened by the green. Better yet, they should move from this somewhat secluded spot.

"Will you walk with me?" He rose and extended his elbow in her direction.

She stood and placed her hand in the crook of his arm. The warmth of her touch sent his mind wandering in another direction, but he quickly reined in his thoughts. It was enough to know he would be escorting such a lovely young lady around town.

Once they had stepped off the green and crossed the street to the sidewalk in front of the shops, he continued. "Our current situation is tenuous at best," he said. "Hostilities have risen to an alarming level. The colonies are continuing to wage war against the French, but they are suffering more loss than gain."

Elanna turned her attention to the storefronts they passed, as if attempting to piece together everything she knew and had learned. "Other than knowing of the disputes, we had no inclination here of how critical the situation had become." She pointed out several new hats in the window of the haberdashery. "Not even our trade has been affected as of yet." She inclined her chin to look at him. "Colonel Washington's journal published in the *Maryland Gazette*, where he shared the details of his encounter with the French near the Great Meadows, was our first indication."

Madison nodded. "The French commander and nine of his men were killed, which led to the colonies rallying in fear of the French threat. Hopefully, we will receive support soon from England." He made a general sweep with his arm to encompass the town. "None of the bloodshed has trickled this far south, which is why I wanted to pay a visit to my family here while I still had the opportunity."

"How soon must you return?"

"I am not sure. I—"

"Special edition! Just arrived! Get the latest *Pennsylvania Gazette.*"

The loud voice of a young lad hawking copies of the *Gazette* prevented Madison from answering Elanna's query. If a special edition had been printed, the news must be of great import. He signaled for the boy and offered a coin for the paper. As soon as the lad continued down the cobblestone street, Madison held the single page in front of him.

Large, black letters shouted, ENGLAND DECLARES WAR ON FRANCE! Dread settled in the pit of his stomach.

Elanna touched the edge of the paper. "They have made it official." Sorrow tinged her words.

He forced himself to look up from the fateful proclamation. Concern was etched in every facet of her delicate face. How could he tell her he had to leave? But he had no choice.

Without thinking, he pulled his arm away and released his hold on the paper. The page fluttered to the ground at their feet. "Miss Hanssen, I must go."

"Go? But must it be so quickly?"

Biting her lip, she bent to stop the paper from blowing across the street in the breeze. He hastily dropped to one knee to help. As they reached for the page, they bumped heads.

Brilliant. He was as couth as a drunken sailor. He smiled, hoping it would soften the abruptness of his announcement, then got to his feet, rubbing his head ruefully. He bent to take her hand, and she rose to stand before him, regarding him gravely.

"Forgive me, Miss Hanssen. Now that England has formally declared war on France, I must return to my post in Boston."

She clutched the paper she had gathered to her bosom. "What will happen?"

Madison wished he knew. "Only time will tell." She started to respond, but he stayed her words with his hand. "I have enjoyed every moment of our conversation, and I do not wish for things to end here." He took a breath and prayed for courage. "Will you write to me?"

"Yes, of course I will," she answered without hesitation.

In spite of the gravity of the military and political situation they faced, a thrill lifted his spirits. He reached into his pouch for paper, but before he could find it, she thrust a small leather-bound booklet tied with twine into his hands, along with a pencil. He raised one eyebrow in question.

She colored prettily. "I keep one of my journals with me at all times."

Yet another facet of this intriguing young lady. Madison knew the significance of what he was about to do, but he could no more resist than he could deny himself food and water. At the thought of the long, solitary journey back to Boston he had before him, he already felt the absence of her company. He quickly scrawled onto one of the blank pages an address where he could be contacted, and prayed her letters would reach him.

With great care, Elanna took the leather-bound journal from him, their hands barely brushing. She clutched the journal to her chest. "I shall write at the earliest opportunity."

Madison lifted her hand to his lips and brushed a kiss across her knuckles. "And I shall eagerly await the receipt of your letter."

He forced himself to turn and stride in the direction of his cousin's home. Unable to avoid a final look, he glanced back over his shoulder to find Elanna watching him.

Sadness softened her features. He gave a cheerful wave and tore his gaze from her as he put more distance between them.

Although hesitant to admit it, he left part of his heart behind.

two

War.

It was such a terrible word. Elanna felt like her every step took her further into a dream. As she watched out the window, the farmhands at work in field and farmyard moved about in a blur. Not even the increased activity in town or the fear that men from home might soon go north to fight pierced her thoughts. She had gone to town often since the day the news arrived. Each day mirrored every other. Folks rushed to and fro, gathering supplies and making preparations, yet Elanna could only think about Madison.

For the first time in her life, someone had treated her with respect and courtesy far beyond her years. Yes, her father and brothers often allowed her to participate in their talks of assembly meetings and other events taking place in the colonies, but there always came a time when they would dismiss her to her chores or refuse to share any details of private meetings. Not only had Madison engaged her in conversation about current events, but he had seemed to appreciate her knowledge, and encouraged it.

"Elanna," her mother's voice interrupted her musings, "are you going to sit in front of that window all morning, or will I benefit from your assistance in preparing the rations for our local friends and neighbors headed north?"

Elanna straightened and blinked several times. Raelene Hanssen was nothing if not hardworking and generous. She expected her children to be the same. Elanna had to focus, had to bring her mind back to the present. There was work to be done, and she needed to be aware enough to complete it. The time wouldn't pass any faster with her daydreaming.

"I'm here, Mama. Tell me what you want me to do."

Mama passed a large wooden bowl down the kitchen table to her. "Separate out the flour into equal portions for the burlap sacks. When you are finished with that, you can move on to the cornmeal."

"Mama, can I help, too?"

"Yes, Mama. Me, too. Please?"

Elanna's younger brother and sister almost tumbled over each other as eight-year-old Divinia missed the step down into the kitchen from the hallway. Nine-year-old Garrick was right on her heels and braced himself on the doorpost to keep from knocking her down. The other two boys, Jerel and Kare, at twelve and thirteen, were already outside with Papa and Edric.

"Garrick, you can go find your papa and help your brothers. You are more than ready to start taking on more responsibility."

"What can I do, Mama?" Divinia clasped her hands in front of her and looked up at Mama with an angelic expression. Elanna's heart warmed at the sight.

"You, my little angel," Mama said as she tapped Divinia's pert nose, "can help me cut pieces of cheesecloth for these canisters."

Mama had often said that children were a sign of God's favor and blessing. And she had a houseful. Elanna hoped she'd be equally blessed when the time came for her to start a family. As she sifted through the flour and portioned out equal amounts for each sack, her mind once again drifted to Madison.

Had he arrived in Boston? Had he received orders to go elsewhere? Did he think of her at all?

Wherever he was, she prayed he was safe. Ever since the news of England's declaration of war, Elanna had been too busy to write even a brief letter to him. And she wanted to have that chance.

⁂

"Wait here. I will go inside and make my way to the window near the back of the hall." Edric crouched next to Elanna at the edge of the bushes lining either side of the town hall. He looked to the left and right and lowered his voice. "I can only raise it a crack, but it should be enough for you to hear what's happening inside."

Elanna pulled her brother toward her in a quick hug. "Thank you."

He cleared his throat and brushed at the collar of his shirt. "If someone finds you, and you get caught, I knew nothing about this."

"I know. And I promise to be careful."

"I do not know why I do these things for you."

"Because you love me," she replied, giving him an impish grin. "And this is not the first time you have risked Papa's punishment."

Winking at her, he said wryly, "Nor will it be the last. Of that, I am certain."

She placed a kiss on his cheek and ducked behind the bushes once more as she made her way to the back of the town hall. Her insides quivered at learning what would be discussed at this emergency meeting of the assembly. No doubt talk of the war would be prevalent, but the decisions that would be made, Elanna had to know. Thanks to Edric, she would find out.

Making sure no one could see her, she moved along the back wall and crept around the corner. Just as she found a somewhat comfortable position, the window right above her head slid open about three inches. A cacophony of voices traveled through the gap. She couldn't make out what any one of them was saying, despite trying to focus on one voice. Too many men were talking over one another.

"This meeting will now come to order!" The assembly speaker's voice rang out above the raucous noise, accompanied by the sound of his gavel.

Elanna placed her fingertips on the windowsill and inched higher until her nose peeked over the edge. Several men in white wigs occupied the seats at the front of the room. The rest of the members sat in the chairs opposite the bar and gate that sectioned off the two areas.

"It is clear that the recent news we have received from England via the *Gazette* has distressed many of us," the speaker began in a somewhat monotone voice. "Although we have not felt the direct effects of the war that has been taking place north and west of us, we are affected nonetheless. As colonies of England, we are obligated to support each other in all matters."

A yawn found its way to Elanna's lips, and she covered her mouth. She hoped this speaker wouldn't be the meeting's primary leader. If so, the honorable members of the assembly would be asleep in no time.

"To aid in the verification of the atrocities being committed against our fellow colonists in the Ohio Valley and Canada, I shall have the clerk to the assembly read personal accounts as reported in various newspapers and publications throughout the colonies." He extended his arm, palm up, toward a young man not much older than Elanna. Her brother had mentioned some of these atrocities. She swallowed and prepared for what the clerk was about to read.

"This appeared in the *Boston Gazette*."

Boston! That was Madison's home. Had he read this before traveling south?

" 'The horrors of the attacks haunt even my waking moments. It is with great difficulty that I write even these words to share with those who may read them. With my own eyes, I saw women and children being taken prisoner, and men brutally beaten or tortured. Acts that I dare not repeat for anyone to read were committed, and the screams of those being persecuted were all for naught. Our friends and brethren, massacred; our fields, laid waste; our territories, possessed by those that hate us.' "

Elanna took several deep breaths to dissipate the bile in her throat. Perhaps this was one of the reasons Papa kept her away from these proceedings. Although not often given to swooning, the reality of the barbaric actions committed by the French and Indians was beyond reason.

The clerk continued. "This is from the *New York Mercury*. 'The French appear to take instruction from the Indians in their violations of the human prisoners they capture. No respect is given, and no mercy is granted in the cruel methods of punishment enacted by the captors. I only pray these atrocities come to an end soon, for I fear the suffering will weaken my fellow colonists and open the door wide to the invasion of the French into our lands.' " With that, the clerk once again took his seat.

Silence settled over the gathered members. Elanna closed her eyes and tried to think of anything but the gruesome images painted by the words the clerk had read. Only the faces of Mama, Papa, and her brothers and sister came to mind. How safe would they be if the French continued their onslaught into British colonial territory?

The speaker once again took the floor. "I have taken the liberty of inviting newly appointed deputy attorney general to County Sussex Thomas McKean, to join us today. He has studied law under Francis Allison and served as clerk to the

Court of Common Pleas. I thought he would best know how to advise us in these circumstances."

The head of the assembly stepped aside and gestured for a young man to take his place. The one identified as Thomas McKean didn't look to have much more than two and twenty years. Atop his hair, pulled back and tied in a pigtail, he sported a powdered wig. Elanna guessed he donned it to add years to his youth, but he only succeeded in appearing foolish. Yet something about the manner in which he carried himself commanded attention and riveted Elanna.

"It is good to see so many of you gathered here today," McKean began, acknowledging the assembly with a graceful wave of his hand. "We are in tumultuous times. While many of our fellow colonists have been engaged in war for nearly two years, we have anxiously been awaiting support from England. It took the publications of fellow colonist Colonel George Washington to alert everyone to the seriousness of the plight to the west of the Appalachians. Now that England has recognized our need and sent the regulars to our aid, it is time for us to act."

"The people here... They are not soldiers. We are merchants and farmers and tradesmen. What help will we bring to the cause?"

Papa! Pride surged through Elanna at hearing her father's voice. He had always held an interest in the assembly, but in recent years, he had become an active member.

Deputy Attorney General McKean didn't appear surprised by the question. With the same command in his voice, he addressed the assembly. "Every man among us can lend aid in many different ways. Although our strengths may lie in areas other than weaponry and taking up arms, our support is critical to the success of this war."

McKean paced across the front of the room. Elanna's legs

ached from her crouched position, but she refused to move. There was no way she would miss a word of this.

"We must take arms against the French and join with our fellow colonists. When our homes and land are threatened, when our enemies plan and execute their barbarous schemes, when all is at stake," he said, pumping the air with each point, "that is when the passions of our hearts must be roused. The time is critical. Our country is in danger, and it needs every one of you. Will you serve?"

A loud chorus of *huzzah*s sounded in response to McKean's challenge. Husbands, fathers, and brothers alike shouted their enthusiastic agreement. Where doubt had been, confidence and determination now showed clear. Elanna almost shouted out as well but managed to keep her emotions in check.

"Is this the manner in which you educate yourself to the happenings throughout the colonies?"

Elanna covered her mouth and swallowed a startled outcry. She whirled so fast at the voice that she lost her balance and would have landed in the bush had it not been for the strong arms that saved her from a fall. With both feet planted on solid ground again, she turned to look up at the interloper. Her heart skipped a beat.

Madison Scott stared down at her with an amused grin on his face. "Or perhaps to gain further information you also play upon the sympathies of innocent soldiers passing through town."

"Major Scott!" At his silent admonition and nod of his head toward the open window, Elanna lowered her voice. "I thought you had returned home to Boston."

He placed a finger to his lips and encouraged her to crouch down next to him against the wall beneath the window. "It was my intention to leave immediately, but upon receiving a summons from the commanding officer of my regiment,

I was given new orders and allocated an additional fortnight before I must join my company."

"And you have been here in town all this time?" How had she not known?

"No, I spent a few days in Philadelphia, speaking with members of the assembly there as well as to others of influence. I needed to gather information that I will take with me on my journey."

"Where are you headed?"

Madison looked away. Regret transformed his face. When he turned toward her again, she could not read the emotion in his eyes. "I am to rejoin my regiment on Lake Champlain in the Hudson Valley."

Elanna inhaled a sharp breath. "But that is in the heart of the war!" she protested. "You will be coming face-to-face with a brutal enemy."

"I know." His jaw hardened as he clenched his teeth, but a soft light also entered his eyes. "As much as it pains me to confirm this with you, it is a necessary part of my duties. Our soldiers need strong leadership. We must remain devoted and dedicated. Otherwise, we will not triumph over our foe."

Beads of sweat formed on his brow. Elanna waved her fan back and forth to ward off the heat of the midday sun and the humidity of the August day. Although grateful that Mama had permitted her to venture into town, wearing only one layer of petticoats, she still felt the trickle of perspiration on her own brow.

"I have a role and a duty in serving with my regiment," he continued in a tense voice. "I want to face the enemy and return the atrocities they have committed against our fellow colonists with equal fervor."

He slammed his fist into the palm of his hand. When Elanna jumped, he lightly enfolded her wrists, remorse dancing across his face.

"Do forgive me, Miss Hanssen. But with each report I read or story I hear, my anger builds to a greater height. I cannot fathom how any man can do what the French and Indians have done to a fellow human being. Their savage behavior must be stopped."

"I am in complete agreement, Major Scott, but at what price?"

He regarded her with admiration shining clear in his eyes. "You are a remarkable young woman, Miss Hanssen."

The warmth of a blush stole across her cheeks, and she dipped her head.

Madison tipped her chin with the lightest of touches, compelling her to meet his earnest gaze. "I am quite sincere in the compliments I bestow. Not only do your social graces hold considerable appeal, but you also possess an intelligent mind and the ability to use it. I find that combination quite. . . laudable."

With every word, he bent toward her, his gaze focused on her lips, until their foreheads almost touched. The heat rose to her cheeks, and the day's oppressive humidity stole her breath.

As though at a great distance, she heard the main door of the town hall creak open and then bang shut. She jumped.

"I owe every bit of my intellect and upbringing to Mama and Papa," she said with a gasp and hastily pulled away from him. "And of course to the good Lord."

"Then they are to be commended as well."

He spoke the words with grim seriousness, an odd expression coming over his face, one Elanna couldn't identify. Before she had time to wonder what he was thinking, he pushed himself erect.

"Walk with me."

It was more of a request than a command, and Elanna complied. The meeting inside had shifted to other assembly matters, and she no longer had any interest in eavesdropping. Accepting his outstretched hand, she rose to her feet and allowed him to escort her from the bushes onto the cleared path that paralleled the town green. He tucked her gloved hand into the crook of his elbow and maintained a respectful distance between them. They walked in silence for several moments. So many things begged to be spoken, but she couldn't find the courage or her voice. Madison saved her the trouble.

"I know the skills which I possess will serve our cause well. It is not without purpose that I have been chosen to serve in the regiment I will soon join." A slight breeze stirred the leaves in the oak and maple trees overhead and sent a welcome coolness across their path. "I have spent many years in preparation for this very thing. Although a part of me would like nothing more than to remain here, I know I am needed in northern New York."

Elanna held in reserve the response her heart wanted her to make and instead maintained a cordial tone. "Your loyalty and devotion alone will serve you well. I have no doubt that men such as yourself are in great need at the heart of this war."

He halted and turned toward her, covering her hand with his. "It is not by chance that our paths have crossed and that I have made your acquaintance, Miss Hanssen."

She nodded. "I believe as you do."

"And I am most sincere in my wish that you write me while I am gone."

At last the conversation turned in the direction she hoped it would go. "It is a request to which I will gladly accede."

His eyes brightened, and a smile tugged at the corners of his lips. He led her across the cobblestone street and onto the town green. "Might I be permitted to offer a confession of sorts to you, Miss Hanssen?"

"Please do, Major Scott."

"Throughout my entire journey southward from Boston, I had the impression that this visit would hold more than time spent with my family and a temporary reprieve from the war."

"And little did I know that I would be so fortunate as to again meet such a charming and affable gentleman. I do pray your service to our fellow colonists will bring great success to their efforts."

Laughter rumbled in his chest. It was such a pleasant sound, and Elanna wanted nothing more than to hear it again and again. A responsive smile formed on her own lips.

"Miss Hanssen, I am certain my time here has only been improved by your presence." He led them to the same stone bench where they had sat two weeks earlier. "I will carry the memory of our time together with me as I journey north to join my regiment."

At the mention of his imminent departure, sadness once again filled his eyes. Elanna sensed his inner struggle. Although his tone and words gave every indication of calm assurance, he seemed to be holding back an urgency he was doing his best to conceal.

He shifted so that his knees touched hers, and he clasped her hands in his. "You have the address where I can be reached."

It was a statement, and not a question, but she nodded to confirm it. "Yes. It is safely tucked away in my desk drawer."

"Might you also provide me with an address to reach you? It is only proper that I initiate our correspondence."

Elanna scribbled the information on a page from her journal, then tore it out and handed it to Major Scott.

"Not only will it afford me the opportunity to ascertain

the safe delivery of our letters, but it will give me a reason to focus on something other than the war at hand."

"I believe that is the wisest path to take," Elanna agreed.

"And you promise you will write in response?"

Hurt crept in that he would doubt her. "Of course. I do not go back on my word."

As if he realized the effect of his words, he capitulated. "Yes, yes. Do forgive me." He paused and again seemed to waver between what he wanted to say and what he would allow himself to say. "I am merely so elated at the prospect of a regular and exceedingly pleasant correspondence while I am away from home fighting, that I had to confirm it. You have been nothing but honest in every way. I shall often call to mind our time together."

"And I shall do the same."

He raised both her hands to his lips and placed a soft kiss on the backs of each, then released them. "Now, I must take my leave before I forget that we have only just met and incur the anger of your father or brothers should I do something untoward."

Elanna quelled the leap of her heart at what his words implied. She snapped open her fan and waved it back and forth to hide her blush.

With an elegant bow, Madison took his leave. "Miss Hanssen. It has been my pleasure."

She nodded. "Major Scott. Godspeed."

And with that, he was gone. Although her heart already missed him, the knowledge that he would carry thoughts of her with him made the parting easier. The time she would spend writing to him would be precious to her.

Six days later, after reading the short missive Major Scott had posted from Philadelphia, Elanna opened the cover of her desk. Retrieving a sheet of parchment from the left drawer, she reached for her quill pen and dipped it in ink, tapping the end on the rim to remove the excess. Her quill hovered over the paper as she contemplated how to begin. Although in her mind, she called him Madison, no intentions had been declared. It was best to keep things formal for now.

Dear Major Scott, she began, and the words flowed from there. After filling several pages inquiring about his journey and sharing responses in town to the news of the war, she ended the letter with a simple, *Miss Elanna Hanssen.*

She only prayed God would keep him safe until the war's end, and that their correspondence would be long and happy.

three

Madison slipped inside his quarters, thankful that his rank guaranteed a private room. The courier had just departed after delivering the mail, and Madison couldn't wait to open the letter he'd received from Elanna. It had been a little over a month since he'd left New Castle. The fighting had gotten off to a slow start. Aside from a few skirmishes and minor attempts to infiltrate the forts near Lake Champlain, not a lot had taken place. He welcomed the diversion Elanna's missive would bring.

After dropping his belt on the floor and leaning his musket against the wall, Madison reclined on the straw tick mattress. With a knife, he slit open the envelope, his heart pounding at what he might find inside. It was dated 12 August 1756, so she must have sat down to write him almost immediately.

Dear Major Scott, it began. Madison's chest fell at the impersonal nature of her greeting. Considering the circumstances, though, he understood. With letters being passed from courier to courier, anyone might intercept them. Had Elanna been anything but formal, word might somehow make its way back to her father, and that would result in consequences neither one of them needed right now. He must find a way to ensure the safe delivery of their letters. Perhaps a single courier he could trust and command on a specific route between the fort and Philadelphia. The short distance to New Castle wouldn't add too much more to the journey.

But he could decide that later. Back to Elanna's letter:

*I hope your journey north was met with favorable winds
and pleasant weather. Having never traveled farther than
Philadelphia, I cannot fathom what sort of conditions you
might encounter on such a trek. From what your cousin
shares with me, provided you stay on the well-traveled roads,
the experience is quite calm.*

*I know, however, that your destination was not to
return home, but instead to venture into the untamed and
uncivilized territory farther west.*

He smiled at how Elanna withheld the specifics of his
location. Despite the informal tone, her concern for him was
evident in the words she chose. It warmed his heart as he read
between the lines and deciphered what she couldn't reveal:

*I have prayed for your safety since your departure. You
will no doubt be relieved to know that I have not engaged in
further eavesdropping escapades since we last spoke. In truth,
I have not found the need, as my brother and father have
agreed to share the news with me following each meeting at
the town hall or gathering of assembly members.*

*I suppose I should inform you that my family is aware of
my correspondence with you. My younger sister, Divinia,
read a part of my letter last night as she was going through
her nightly routine and informed Mama, who called me
to the parlor. I told them of your family relation to Chelcy.
They are aware that we met while I was visiting in town
and that you requested to be kept informed of our lives here.
Papa seemed satisfied with my explanation, but Mama
looked as if she wanted to question me further. She no doubt
believes there is more to our correspondence, but I assured her
otherwise. Thankful for the late hour, I pleaded fatigue and
excused myself to my room.*

At least Elanna's family was aware of their acquaintance, but she left out their two meetings in private and stressed friendship to her mother. Was friendship all she truly felt? Or had she only been careful in her parents' presence?

Madison regretted not having spoken with her father or any other members of her family. He and Elanna must still maintain extreme caution regarding the content of their letters, but with her family's blessing, they would be free to continue their friendship.

I do not know what sort of challenges you have encountered at your present location, but I pray you are protected and that you take care to avoid foolish endeavors that might jeopardize your safety. It is exciting to have a reason to write this letter, and I would be quite disappointed should something happen to you that would put an end to our written exchange. There is so much to tell you, I hardly know where to begin.

Activity in town has increased in a way that I have never seen before. We have travelers from the two counties below us and even visitors from across the river. All of them appear to be in a great hurry, whatever their mission. Just the other day, I encountered an elderly gentleman dressed in the latest fashion and finest clothing who held an air of importance about him. He and Mr. McKean appeared to be acquainted with each other, and the two men spent quite a bit of time together. I wonder if he might be someone from one of the southern counties, as they both met with the assembly. But what struck me the most was the kindness in his eyes. Despite the obvious critical nature of his business, he took the time to speak to passersby and tip his hat to acknowledge every lady who crossed his path. Now, I regret not inquiring about his identity, for he might be someone of great import to these counties.

Madison tried to recall the names of notable men residing in New Castle and Kent counties. From Elanna's mention of this gentleman's acquaintance with Deputy Attorney General McKean, he suspected the man might be either the high sheriff of Kent County, Caesar Rodney, or prominent New Castle lawyer, George Read. Both men were heavily involved in the political direction of their counties and had both been present in Philadelphia during his visit. Because of his position as liaison to the Boston Assembly and by brief assignment in Philadelphia, he would not soon forget those names. Whomever Elanna had seen, she would no doubt see more of him as this war progressed.

Yet again, Madison brought his attention back to the letter he held. Although he wanted to remain focused, Elanna's words sent his thoughts running in several different directions.

As you will know from that detail, I returned to town just two days following your departure. Mama and I, along with my younger sister, needed to purchase some supplies and materials in preparation for the upcoming harvest and winter. No matter how often I come to town, I am always struck by the variety of shops that line both sides of the town green and the activity down by the river. There have been times when I have stolen moments alone with my journal along the riverbanks. Although there are many places on my family's land where I can go, I find the river's solitude to be quite a refreshment and inspiration to the writings in my journal.

There is something about the larger ships that travel the waters, or even the smaller fishing vessels and steamboats, that gives me a sense of connection to the great world beyond the horizon. And when I accompany Mama visiting the various shops in town, I realize just how important are the people who work as tradesmen and skilled artisans, from the milliner to the blacksmith. Each one is a key part of the web woven among all of us.

Elanna had such a way with words. Madison could picture everything just as she described it. He remembered passing the shops that she mentioned during their walk. They had pondered the fate of certain merchants, and now, being on the front lines of the war, he revisited those questions in his mind.

But I am no doubt boring you with such sentimental musings. With your rank, you must have more important things to attend to than spending time reading this rather wordy missive. It is time I brought this letter to a close. I pray it reaches you safely and that you send a reply as soon as you are able.

Sincerely,
Miss Elanna Hanssen

He stared at the last page for several moments, then read the entire letter again, before folding it and returning it to its envelope. A knock at his door interrupted his solitude.

"Enter." He slipped Elanna's letter into the drawer of the stand next to his bed and stood to greet the visitor.

Lieutenant Matthew Lewis ducked under the doorframe as he stepped across the threshold. "Major Scott."

"Lieutenant." Madison nodded.

"I have a summons from the colonel. He said he needs to see you immediately in the East Magazine."

"Thank you, Lieutenant."

Lewis tipped his head toward the drawer. "Was that a letter from a young lady?"

Madison looked from the wooden stand to his compatriot.

Mirth sparkled in Lewis's eyes.

"You disappeared quick as lightning, even before the courier had a chance to exit the fort. I knew it had to be from someone special."

Madison dropped the regimental pretenses. Facing Matthew as the friend that he'd become since their arrival, Madison allowed a grin to form on his lips.

"Yes. We met during my recent visit to New Castle and Philadelphia." He was careful not to reveal too much. "She is a close friend of my cousin, and we developed a rapport sharing news of the developments in the war. Her father is a member of the assembly there, so she is kept informed."

"I suspect she is something more to you than a friend," Matthew countered.

Madison regarded Matthew for a moment. He should have known better than to try and hide something from the perceptive lieutenant. Lewis had a keen eye and observant nature that served him well in his role as a scout for the fort.

"It is impossible to hide anything from you."

Lewis grinned. "You are not very good at telling falsehoods. Besides, there are only two reasons a soldier disappears as fast as you did. One is a letter from family. The other is a letter from a special lady."

Madison knew when he'd been beaten. "All right, yes. She is special to me. As things stand now, though, I cannot say if there is a future for us. I am happy knowing she cares enough to write."

"I would feel the same. Does she have any eligible sisters?"

The gleam in Lewis's eyes couldn't be missed. Madison clapped him on the shoulder and turned him toward the doorway. "Even if she did, I would never subject them to your merciless torment."

Clearly not put off by the rebuff, Lewis held his ground.

"Ah, so none are eligible. How about your young cousin, then?"

"She is already spoken for."

Lewis shrugged. "You cannot blame a man for trying."

"No, but I can requisition your current nonrestrictive scout post to be reassigned due to insubordination toward a superior officer."

"You would never do that, and we both know it," Lewis returned as he stepped outside. "You be sure and find me if you hear of an eligible young lady through the letters of your lady friend." With that, he vanished, and only sunlight filled the space he had just occupied.

Madison chuckled as he repaired his uniform in preparation for facing the colonel. Details of Elanna's letter replayed themselves in his memory and helped buoy his spirits, despite the perilous situation that faced everyone at the fort each day on this frontier.

૨૪

Scents of spices, fresh vegetables, and roast chicken permeated every corner of the Hanssen farmhouse. Harvest was Elanna's favorite time of year. The temperatures remained cool enough to require a wrap and invigorating when spending time outdoors. Inside, she and Mama and Divinia, along with several servants, stayed busy with the food preparation, baking, and cleaning. After starting before dawn, Elanna had the chance for a break when the sun passed the highest point in the sky.

"Mama, Edric is taking the wagon to the Cooper farm north of town. He has offered to take me with him so I can visit with Chelcy. May I go?" Elanna shifted from one foot to the other, praying Mama would agree.

"Have the harvested grains been sifted and separated?"

"Yes, ma'am."

"Did you gather the apples that were picked this morning?"

"I just finished," she replied and continued without missing a beat. "And I have also rolled out the dough for the pies and prepared the spices for the cider."

Mama laughed. "By all means, then. Go with your brother." She pointed a flour-covered finger at Elanna. "But mind your manners at the Greysons' and while you are in town. I do not wish to hear of any more of your adventurous jaunts at the next ladies' auxiliary luncheon."

Elanna ducked her head and stared at the wooden floor. At least Mama only referred to the last visit to town when Chelcy dared Elanna to climb the wide oak at one end of the green just to see how high she would go. She had been concealed by the tree's brilliant red leaves, but Mrs. Whipple—the leader of the wagging tongues in town—happened upon their private escapade and nearly suffered a case of the vapors at the sight of Elanna high in a tree.

"I promise, Mama." She stepped forward and kissed Mama's cheek, then grabbed her shawl and went in search of Edric.

❧

"You finally received a second letter, and you could not even wait two days before writing a reply?" Chelcy poured tea for Elanna and herself, then took the empty seat across the table from her friend in the Greysons' elegant garden. "Do you not fear that he will find you too eager?"

Elanna hadn't considered that possibility. She raised the teacup to her lips and sipped the hot liquid, taking a moment to collect her thoughts. "I was careful to remain polite and formal in every word of my letter."

With ornate silver tongs, Chelcy cut a generous portion from the cone of sugar and stirred it into her tea. She pursed her lips as she waited for the sugar to dissolve.

"So you withheld any personal details and simply informed Madison of our little local events as you would a complete stranger?"

"No!" Elanna protested, almost spilling the liquid in her cup. She took two deep breaths and continued. "I simply made certain that he would know how much I value this opportunity to write to him, but as we spent so little time together, there was nothing definite to convey."

"Yet the pink in your cheeks says otherwise," Chelcy teased.

Elanna touched the warm spots and smiled. "Can I help it if your cousin is the most charming gentleman I have met in some time?"

"What about Samuel Hall?"

The earnest face of the young man who had made it a point to shadow Elanna's every step whenever they were in town at the same time appeared in her mind's eye. "He is attentive, I will admit."

"I would think besotted is a better word."

"You only enjoy chiding me because you have your future secure with your betrothal to Mr. James Wythe."

A faraway look appeared on Chelcy's face, and she sighed. "Yes, I do have a wonderful young man who adores me. We have known each other since the day he threw a snowball that accidentally hit the back of my head."

Elanna sighed as well and placed the back of her hand against her forehead. "Such a romantic start to a lifelong friendship."

They both laughed, and the shared moment lifted Elanna's spirits. She only wished she didn't have to wait for the infrequent visits to town to see her friend.

"I do not know how I will wait another two years before we can wed."

"The same way I will wait until I can see your cousin again."

Chelcy brightened at this. "Ah yes, I had almost forgotten the focus of our conversation this afternoon."

"At least you have Mr. Wythe here in town to make the waiting more bearable."

"I thought you said you were only attracted to Madison for his charm?"

Elanna's heart skipped a beat. She opened her mouth to counter Chelcy's acuity, but it was no use. "I must confess. Despite my words to the contrary, your cousin made quite an impression on me during his brief visit. It has been two months, and I cannot stop thinking about him." She took a final sip of tea. "Every day, I find myself watching for the courier to see if he will stop at our farm with a missive for me. And every day, I am disappointed all over again."

"You only wrote him again three weeks ago." Chelcy reached across the table and covered one of Elanna's hands with her own. "It takes a long time for letters to make their way to their destination." She sat back and gave her a pointed look. "And you yourself told me he did not know for certain when he would reach Fort Edward."

"I pray for him every day, wondering where he is and what he is doing, if he is in the middle of a battle or safe inside the fort." She stared into her teacup, its emptiness an equal companion to her soul.

"Do you feel like something untoward has befallen Madison?"

"Of course not." And Elanna prayed she was right.

"Then trust God has him safe and protected and that only the war is keeping him from writing."

Elanna didn't know what she would do without Chelcy's friendship. Although Mama had a special way of knowing just when she needed encouragement, Chelcy managed to help keep Elanna's head focused on what was important.

"Now, tell me what it is about my cousin that has you so addlepated?"

Elanna moved her teacup and saucer to the side and dropped

her chin into her hand, elbow propped on the table. "What about him would *not*?"

"Oh no." Chelcy offered an exaggerated look of remorse. "You are suffering from an acute case of infatuation. Did I not warn you the day you met him to be careful?"

"Yes, but he was every bit the gentleman that day. I was merely flattered. It was the second time I saw him that made his leave-taking more difficult than I would have imagined."

"Wait a minute." Chelcy placed both hands on the table. "You saw him again? How did I not know about this?"

Elanna furrowed her brows. "Did I not tell you?" Surely she hadn't forgotten such an important detail.

"No, and you should be tarred and feathered for neglecting that important piece of information!"

"He caught me eavesdropping at the assembly meeting where deputy attorney general Thomas McKean was invited to speak."

Chelcy covered her mouth to hide the laugh that erupted at Elanna's confession. "Where were you hiding?"

"In the bushes near the back of the town hall. Edric raised a window so I could hear."

"And did Madison mete out the appropriate form of punishment for your infraction?"

Heat crept up Elanna's neck, but it didn't warm her cheeks. "He chastised me, but then we went for a walk. The meeting had almost come to an end by that time, anyway."

A servant girl came from the house and removed the dishes from their afternoon tea. Elanna looked through the wrought-iron gate leading to the street and caught sight of Edric arriving with the wagon. She stood, and Chelcy did the same.

"Edric has returned, so I must leave."

Chelcy came around the table and enfolded Elanna's hands

in her own. "You must find an excuse to visit me more often. I wish to hear more about your letters to my cousin and, when he responds, how he is faring."

"I will do my best. Winter is upon us, though, so our visits to town will be reduced."

"Then I shall be happy with whatever you are able to share with me." She gave Elanna a hug. "Godspeed, my dear friend."

Elanna returned the hug. "And the same to you."

As she sat beside Edric for the ride home, she was thankful he was the quieter of the two of them. Her mind wandered toward Madison again. This afternoon had cheered her, but she still hadn't received any word from Fort Edward. If only Madison would write!

four

"You are certain you wish to continue your involvement with the assembly, yes?"

Elanna sat at the table, husking ears of corn, as her father, Gustaf Hanssen, spoke with Edric. Despite the sixteen years since he and Mama wed, a hint of his Swedish ancestry still remained in the lilt to his voice and choice of words.

"Yes, sir. I have never been more certain."

"You are an excellent listener and have a sharp mind. It will take you far with this goal."

"Thank you, sir. I have learned from watching you."

Elanna smiled and tossed another husk into the pail at her feet. Such praise would guarantee that Papa would consider Edric's request. She hoped her brother succeeded. The information she desired would be right at her fingertips. Edric would make sure of that.

"Very well," Papa announced. "I will petition the assembly when next we meet and ask that they make you a clerk to the assembly until you reach eighteen years. At that time, if your service has been without reproach, you will be invited to become a member." He paused, and Elanna glanced to the side to see Papa place his hand on Edric's shoulder. "Until that time, and with the agreement of the assembly, you will attend every meeting and write notes on everything that is discussed. This is to include meetings at the town hall and any gatherings at the homes of assembly members. You will know of these before they happen."

Elanna had not often heard Papa so serious, but she

understood the important role the assembly played in regard to their political well-being and their protection. If Edric didn't grasp the significance, his future with the assembly would be short-lived. Elanna kept her attention on Papa and Edric even as she continued her task.

"You will share equal duty with reports to the assembly on what was discussed at meetings before. It is most important when not all members were present. Do you approve of this?"

"Yes, sir." Edric stood erect and placed a fist over his chest as he faced Papa. "Should the assembly accept my request, I pledge my troth that I will endeavor to do all that is asked of me." He relaxed and looked Papa square in the eyes. "I will not disappoint you, Papa."

Papa smiled. "Of that, I am certain, my son." He ruffled Edric's hair and gave him a solid thump on his back.

Mama wiped her hands on her apron and regarded the two men with pride shining in her eyes. She didn't get as involved as Elanna in the political discussions, but she knew what was happening. Elanna remembered the stories Mama would tell about first coming to the colonies at age fourteen, and how she believed she would never be happy away from England. When she lost her parents three years later, her desolation had been complete. But she made up her mind to make the family farm a success, despite turning her back on God. Then she met Papa, and everything changed. Elanna smiled at the memory. Mama resisted, at first, but God and Papa eventually won. Even then, Mama was determined to know everything and be kept informed.

"Your inquisitive nature comes to you naturally," Mama once whispered in Elanna's ear, after one of the ladies in town had chided her for talking out of turn.

Elanna knew this to be true. No doubt, it was why she wasn't often reprimanded for her questions or desire to be involved. As she grew older, Mama taught her when to ask questions and when to listen. That virtue had served her well and opened many doors.

"Are you finished with the corn, Elanna?"

Mama's voice broke into her thoughts. She looked at the final ear in her hand. The husk had already been removed and discarded into the pail.

"Yes, Mama. I am sorry. I was daydreaming again."

"Probably about the handsome knight who will ride up on his great, white steed and carry you off into the sunset," Edric teased.

Elanna stuck out her tongue at her brother, and he laughed.

"That is enough, you two." Mama returned to her work in front of the fire. "So long as you complete your chores, Elanna, you may daydream as much as you wish."

Elanna gave Edric a triumphant grin and stuck her chin in the air. Edric grimaced and followed Papa into the hall. They, along with Jerel and Kare, still had work to do before sundown. At any moment, Divinia and Garrick would no doubt burst through the back door from the barn after they finished feeding the livestock. Soon they would all share supper together and the day would be complete. Elanna couldn't remember feeling more blessed.

❧

"Look what I have, Elanna!" Edric called as he ran up the stone path to the house.

Elanna knelt in front of the flower bed, pulling out the last of the weeds. It wouldn't be long before the first frost, and she was glad. She didn't relish this chore in the least. Sometimes, Divinia helped, and the two made a game of it to see who could pull out the most weeds. But Mama had Divinia inside today, teaching her how to bake pies.

When Edric came to a sudden halt in front of her, Elanna

deigned to glance up, her lips pursed. "You have what?"

He waved a newspaper in front of her. "The first edition of the *Wilmington Journal*. It is new—right off the press." When she reached for it, he snatched it away from her grasp.

Calmly resuming her chore, she feigned disinterest. "Very well. If you insist on these childish games."

As she had known he would, Edric lowered the paper. "Aw, Elanna, I was just teasing."

Elanna snatched the paper out of his unwary hands and laughed. He folded his arms. "And you accuse *me* of being childish."

Elanna shrugged and spread the paper across her knees. "It gained me success, did it not?" she retorted with a grin.

"I fail to understand why you are so eager to devour every tidbit of news about the war."

She scanned the articles on the front page. Two jumped out at her. Unlike the *Pennsylvania Gazette*, this newspaper appeared to be highly critical of the British conduct of the war.

Reluctantly dragging her eyes away from the page, she looked up at Edric before reading. "Do you not care about what might happen to us if the French succeed in their ambitions? Our livelihoods, our freedoms, our very lives are at stake!"

He straightened, back erect. "How can you ask that of me? You were there when I pledged my troth to honor my duties with the assembly and serve them with vigilance."

"Then my interest in the outcome of this war should not surprise you."

"But you cannot—"

"Cannot what?" she interrupted, eyes narrowed. When Edric looked away and didn't respond, she demanded. "Cannot fight? Does that make me any less able to serve?"

"That is not what I intended to say."

She stood and faced her brother, hand on her hip. "Then what, pray tell, did you intend?"

"Aw, sis, I cannot bear it when you are cross with me." Edric offered an apologetic grin. "I only meant that it is not common to find a young woman with so much interest in a war that is not even being fought near our hometown."

"But it *is* being fought right here! Have you not noticed the change in town in regard to trade? The cost of many items has risen because we can no longer get them as easily as before." She flicked the paper in her hand with one finger. "Because we are at war with the French, the goods they used to provide to us are no longer available, nor can we trade our goods with them."

Edric pursed his lips. "You are right, of course."

"Since your ambition is to serve in the assembly, you need to be aware of *all* the effects of this war."

"Then it is a good thing I have you for a sister." He chucked her chin. "What would I do without you?"

Elanna grinned. "Perish from embarrassment when it becomes obvious that you do not stay abreast of political issues."

A bellowing laugh burst forth from his chest. "You will never allow that to happen. Of that, I am certain." Edric stepped past her. "Now, I shall leave you to your reading." He leaned in close to her ear. "But I am also certain there is no mention of your Major Scott in those articles."

It took two seconds for Elanna to realize what Edric had said. She whirled on him just in time to give him a solid shove in the direction of the house. His laughter rang out long after he had disappeared inside. She couldn't be angry with him, though. Far too many times, he had helped her to gain access to things she never would have had without his assistance. Having him know about her interest in Madison wouldn't hurt anyone. If anything, Edric might keep an ear out for specific news.

She retrieved Madison's letter from its place tucked into the waist of her overskirt. Already showing signs of wear from the many times she had folded and unfolded the paper to read it, the brief words he'd written remained imprinted on her mind:

1 October 1756
Dear Miss Hanssen,

I apologize for how long it has taken me to write this letter and send it on its way to you. The situation here is not as we had been led to believe, which has occasioned this delay. However, be assured that we officers are doing everything in our power to keep the morale of our men high. You will be glad to know that our provincial troops perform with admirable gallantry and determination.

Receiving your first letter lifted my spirits in spite of the difficult circumstances that face us here every day. Although we have yet to suffer a direct attack on our fort, the battles and skirmishes are not far away and we feel their effects here. We have often been called upon to send detachments to support the other regiments nearby. I have personally led units of militia into the throes of battle, and more than once, we have suffered losses that sap us of hope for a speedy and positive conclusion to this war.

Whenever I feel my optimism waning, I have only to pull out your letter and read it again. From your description, I feel as if I am right there with you and long to be so. Your words buoy me when I am at my lowest and offer a too brief reprieve from the burden of the responsibility we have assumed. Knowing that you think of us here and take the time to write gives me a reason to fight with renewed vigor. Even when we learn another fort has fallen into the hands of our enemy, the goal we have set out to achieve and the prayers of our friends and families inspire us to press forward. Our losses might increase, but our fortitude is greater yet.

I trust this letter finds you in continued good health, and that the effects of this war have not altered your life in too drastic a way. I only wish we would soon see the end to this fighting, but I fear that is yet a long way off. Please continue to write when you are able. Until such time as I can return a message, take comfort in knowing I think of you often.

Yours sincerely,
Major Madison Scott

Elanna pressed the letter to her bosom and closed her eyes. If she concentrated hard enough, she could almost feel the touch of his hand upon hers and hear the sound of his voice. Duplicating the care she took to conceal any specifics about his location and activities, Madison had still managed to convey considerably more than he was able to detail with his words.

That thought brought her attention back to the *Wilmington Journal.* The articles confirmed what Madison had implied in his letter. She sent up a silent prayer that the major would successfully continue to protect the provincial forces amid the Indian attacks. Her prayer concluded, she read further, noting that the journalist was named Arthur Witherspoon.

Wilmington was only six miles from New Castle, she reminded herself. Papa had told her about the original settlement and how the Dutch took control from the Swedes, after which the British wrested control from the Dutch.

"Much like New Castle," she remarked to herself.

The year Mama and Papa wed was the same year King George II granted Wilmington a borough charter, changing its name from Willington. Now shipbuilding was a key industry.

"And Mr. Arthur Witherspoon lives right in the middle of it all," she mused. "I believe I shall find a way to make his acquaintance."

With determination in her step, Elanna went in search of Papa. If he agreed and escorted her for the initial meeting, perhaps Edric would be able to accompany her on all future visits. Her parents encouraged her quest for knowledge. Speaking with a newspaper writer would be the best resource anyone could find.

੨੦

Edric guided the team along the cobblestone street and brought them to a stop outside the print shop on the northwest corner of Eleventh and Market Streets. Elanna once again marveled at the small board sign swinging from a bracket above the door of a weathered, red-brick building, announcing the structure as the office of the *Wilmington Journal.* It had taken her by surprise on her first visit. Although the meeting had only lasted a few minutes, Papa had seemed satisfied that the journalist was an upstanding gentleman who could be trusted. Today, Elanna would learn more.

She took in her surroundings with amazement. It was hard to believe a town established after New Castle had grown so quickly. Only a short distance north, yet leagues ahead of her hometown in development and industry.

Edric turned to her, hesitation written on his face. "You are certain about speaking with this man who writes for the *Journal*?"

Elanna placed a reassuring hand on his arm and smiled. "You know Papa has already granted his permission. I only wish to find out if Mr. Witherspoon has any connections to someone closer to the fighting. Judging from the articles he publishes, he must have sources outside of Wilmington and even Philadelphia." She glanced up at the two-story brick building. "I do not want to have to wait for the next edition to be printed before learning the most current news."

"I suspect your true purpose is to find out more about your Major Scott. . .and find out whether he is safe," Edric added with a twinkle in his eyes.

Did everyone know of her interest in the dashing major? She thought she had been careful to conceal her feelings. Then again, they *were* her family, and family noticed everything.

As though he read her thoughts, Edric patted her hand. "Do not worry. Your secret is safe with me. Papa and Mama like him and approve of your writing to him."

Elanna conceded a wry smile. "Yes, but they could easily devise more if you say anything. Promise me you will not breathe a word."

He looked wounded. "Of course. You are my sister, after all, and naturally I have your best interests at heart. Nor do I wish to run afoul of your notable temper."

"Edric!" Elanna slapped him on the arm with the rolled-up newspaper she clutched in her hands.

"And you have proven my point." Giving her a smug smile, he climbed down from the wagon, then with a flourish offered his hand to help her alight. "Now, let us see if this man is available for us to call upon him."

Elanna walked next to him up the stone path to the print shop door and followed him inside. The room they entered took up the dilapidated building's entire first floor, but it was illuminated only by the light from a couple of small windows and a single lantern.

As she had just come from the bright outdoors, it took a moment for Elanna's eyes to adjust to the shop's relative gloom. When they did, her gaze first focused on a large printing press that occupied the room's center. Except for racks of type and shelves against the damp-stained walls that held newsprint and ink, the space was sparsely furnished.

After a moment, she became aware of a slender, well-built man standing at a table beside the press with his back to them. It appeared he had been placing rows of lead type into a framework of some sort. His impeccable dress proclaimed him a gentleman. At the moment, however, he was in his shirtsleeves, which were rolled up above his elbows to expose his forearms. From the bulge of his muscles, Elanna judged that he was not given to indolence.

When the man turned, Elanna gasped. It was the journalist. His eyes showed his recognition of her, and he smiled. "So nice to see you again, Miss Hanssen," he said with a brief bow before turning to face Edric and extending his hand. "Good day! I am Arthur Witherspoon. How may I be of service?"

Edric reached to respond in like kind, but his hand stopped abruptly in midair. Taken aback, Witherspoon glanced down at his ink-smudged fingers then withdrew his hand with a rueful chuckle.

He enfolded his hands in the apron tied over his clothing to wipe away the ink with a sigh. "I apologize profusely. I am discovering that printing is a messy business in more ways than one." Dropping the edge of the apron, he again extended his hand.

With a laugh, Edric shook his hand, then stepped back to include Elanna. "I am Edric Hanssen, and this is my sister, Elanna, whom you have already met. She is the one who wishes to talk with you. She is quite interested in learning more about the articles you write on the war."

Witherspoon didn't bother to conceal his surprise. Their first meeting hadn't allowed much time for more than an exchange of formalities, and she hadn't been able to observe him in his work clothes. Today, he appeared younger than Elanna had originally surmised, only a few years older than she and Edric, she guessed. His clothing was tailored to perfection, indicating that he came from a family of influence.

"I must say that I do not often find myself conversing with young ladies about war or about journalism," he said with a smile as he bowed over top of her gloved hand. "I am intrigued. How does a lady of quality such as yourself develop an interest in such matters?"

A great deal of charm partnered with an expression of genuine sincerity in his eyes. Elanna couldn't tell if she could trust him, but she intended to find out.

"My father and brother are both involved with the assembly in New Castle, and my mother not only has a keen interest in political issues but has also made certain I am well informed about everything that affects us in one way or another."

"Quite commendable." He turned toward the narrow staircase at the hallway's far end and extended his arm toward them both. "Will you both accompany me upstairs to my office? We can talk further in greater comfort there."

❧

Madison looked around the infirmary at the long rows of wounded soldiers who had been brought into the fort following the latest battle. It made his stomach turn to see some with missing limbs, others with more bandages than clothing, and some who had been given a hopeless prognosis. The latter were being made as comfortable as possible until death finally won.

Unable to bear any more of the wretched scene, he slipped outside to the parade ground, where he caught sight of a courier speaking with the colonel. It was a different man from the last one who had delivered Elanna's letter, and it occurred to him that perhaps a bargain could be made with the young lad. Unwilling to interrupt the conversation, he headed toward the main gate. A part of him wanted to see if another letter waited for him, but he reined in his anticipation.

Ten minutes later, the courier stepped away from the colonel and turned toward the main gate. He halted when Madison stepped forward from the shadows.

"Major," the young man greeted with a nod.

"Madison Scott," he replied and held out his hand.

"Benjamin Hendricks, sir."

Madison nodded toward where the colonel was disappearing inside the barracks with a satchel of mail. "Is that the latest mail from Boston?"

"As well as New York and Philadelphia. Yes, sir."

"What happened to the last courier?"

The lad shifted the remaining satchel on his shoulder. "He was assigned to a different route."

This could work out better than Madison had thought. "So, you will be delivering the mail from now on?"

Benjamin regarded him with a curious lift to his brow. "As long as I am needed and, of course, provided I remain alive to continue."

The reminder of the danger for everyone on the frontier, regardless of their form of service, strengthened Madison's resolve. He had to have a guarantee of connection with Elanna, even if he had no promise for tomorrow.

"Was there something you wanted?" Benjamin prodded.

"As a matter of fact, yes." Now, how could Madison phrase this in such a way as to not arouse suspicion or invite unwelcome questions? "I have a proposition for you. Should you agree, I will make it a command to ensure that you endure no questions about your duties." Benjamin nodded, and Madison continued. "Before my assignment here, I was visiting family in the lower counties of Pennsylvania. Upon news of my departure, I swore to maintain communication and keep my family informed of war developments. I also have important information to share with several assembly members in Philadelphia."

"And how can I assist you in this?"

"If you would be willing to ensure delivery of all letters I send with you and make certain that all letters coming to me are safely placed in my hands, I would make it worth your while."

Benjamin drew his eyebrows together. "You are aware that any official business is delivered posthaste and given the utmost priority."

Madison's breath caught in his throat for a second. "Yes, but this is not official military business. . .at least not in the manner you are thinking."

A slight upturn to Benjamin's mouth preceded a knowing gleam in his eyes. "Ah, so you wish me to deliver your letters to a young lady back home, then, in addition to the official messages to Philadelphia."

Madison didn't know whether to smile at being found out or maintain his charade. If he was going to take Benjamin into his confidence, he should do so with a clear conscience.

"Yes, but our correspondence is also between our families. It is imperative that—"

Benjamin held up a hand to stay any further explanation. "Say no more. I correspond with a young lady myself, and I only see her on my return trips to New York. I am more than aware of your plight, and I would be honored to undertake such a mission." He smiled. "Who knows? Perhaps assisting you and your young lady will help make my separation from Isabelle easier to bear."

"I cannot tell you how grateful I am." Madison reached into his pouch and withdrew a coin. "Here is something to send you on your way."

"Thank you." Benjamin took the payment and started to turn again toward the gate but grinned at Madison instead. "Oh, and you will find a letter addressed to you in the satchel I delivered today." With a salute, he left.

"Godspeed!" Madison called to his back.

As soon as the doors of the fort closed behind Benjamin, Madison cut a quick path to the general barracks in search of his coveted letter from Elanna. Although tenuous, the vow from the courier gave him an added measure of hope. If only negotiations in the war progressed as easily.

five

The wind howled outside, and drafts crept through the cracks around the window in Madison's quarters. Despite the stone walls of the fortification, the cold still seeped in through even the slightest nook or cranny. With temperatures falling to below freezing and the ground covered with a solid layer of snow, the soldiers sought refuge and warmth wherever they could. Only two days until Christmas, and morale at the fort continued to sink. Madison burrowed further under the bear hide that their Iroquois scout, Tehonawaga, had given him.

It was difficult, at times, to fight against certain of the Indian tribes when others were allies of the British. The soldiers were thankful for every bit of aid they received, though, especially in a land so foreign to many of them. As they trekked back to the fort following the attacks he led, Madison often became even more intensely aware of the miles that separated them from any form of civilization.

He huddled near the recessed hole in the wall that served as a fireplace. From time to time, he roused to poke at the burning logs. Sparks leaped off the wood and crackled as they floated upward. Flames licked at the sticks and twigs, increasing in ferocity as they devoured the logs. Heat radiated from the fire, although it did little to penetrate to the deeper parts of Madison's body where the cold had reached. Still, it kept his teeth from chattering.

Fire had always fascinated him. One could create a blaze with just a spark from a flint and tinder, and the vivid blue amid the yellow, red, and orange when the fire reached its hottest point amazed him. He had always wondered what type of trade he'd learn once his military service was over. His father had always maintained that Madison possessed uncommon skill with iron. That could lead him to the trade of blacksmithing, or perhaps he might move to Wilmington and get involved with the shipbuilding industry Elanna had written about in her last letter:

> *You would be intrigued by the process of shipbuilding and all of the intricacies that go into making a ship seaworthy. Mr. Witherspoon took me down to the river, where I stood mesmerized at the shell of a ship and imagined what it would look like when it was complete. When I spoke with one of the workers, he told me that the ships they build there either go farther north to the port in Philadelphia or travel southward to other harbors along the coastline.*
>
> *Imagine, Madison, what it might be like to be on board a ship such as those and float along the water, going wherever the current might take you.*

Madison recalled those lines as easily as he could those verses in his well-worn Bible that he'd memorized as a young lad. But the last line stuck out more than the others because it was the first time Elanna had used his given name and not referred to him as Major Scott. Although the familiarity of using her first name came so easy to him in his thoughts, he would continue to address her as Miss Hanssen. The war offered little assurance that they would meet again, and he didn't want to raise her hopes only to have them dashed should something happen to him.

Elated that Elanna had befriended a journalist who would keep her informed on the progress and details of the war, Madison decided to compose a reply. Rising to his knees, he reached for the inkwell and a piece of paper and brought them down to the smooth stone hearth. As he dipped the quill into the ink and started to write the greeting, voices just outside his quarters interrupted him. A knock followed a moment later.

"Major Scott, are you in there?"

It was Lieutanant Lewis.

"Come in, Matthew!" Madison called through the closed door.

A blast of cold air accompanied Matthew's entrance, and he quickly shut out the frigid invasion. Stomping his boots to, no doubt, attempt to return feeling to his feet, the lieutenant pulled his own pelt tight around him before facing Madison.

"Most of the soldiers have gathered in the main hall, and many of them have set up pallets on the floor where they sleep."

Madison chuckled. "Attempting to find a better way to keep warm?"

"It appears that way."

"And what about you. Have you done the same?"

Matthew shook his head. "I wanted to come and see what you would do. With Christmas just two days away and a lot of us wishing we were anywhere but here, I thought it might raise morale if we all assembled in one place. Misery loves company, you know," he concluded with a grin.

Madison saw where Matthew was headed. "We might as well become family to each other when we do not have our own here to celebrate with us?"

"Exactly. I already spoke with the colonel, and he agreed that it might help boost spirits. We are not likely to see any fighting in the coming weeks."

"At least not until the ice melts and allows passage through the waterways." They could be grateful to the cold for that reprieve. Madison stood and returned the inkwell and paper to his desk, then readjusted the bearskin and faced Matthew again. "I thought I would spend the entire winter here in these quarters and pass the time writing letters." He chuckled. "But I find your suggestion much more to my liking."

Matthew laughed as he yanked open the door and preceded Madison into the corridor. Grabbing what belongings he might need and stopping by Matthew's quarters to allow his friend do the same, Madison followed the lieutenant down the drafty stairwell. Their footsteps echoed in the cavernous passageway, a fitting parallel to the echo in his soul at being apart from family during the winter months. At least he had his friends.

⋙

Madison pushed himself erect from where he had been leaning on the rampart walls and forced himself to pace along the narrow walkway, hoping to keep his legs from going numb. He glanced every so often over the outer wall into the whirling snow that had started falling just after midnight last night, adding inches to the foot already on the ground. How he had ended up in command of the evening watch on Christmas, he didn't know, but he might as well make the best of it.

While striding along, he looked over the wall. Something caught his eye. His whole body tensed, and he blinked several times to get a clear view. If he didn't know better, he'd swear that someone was approaching the fort. From Madison's vantage point, it looked like he was carrying a large load on his shoulders. As Madison watched, the figure came closer to the fort. There was no doubt in his mind, now. Some fool had braved this treacherous weather. He only prayed the fool was friend, not foe.

Deciding against ringing the bell and alerting everyone,

Madison went in search of two soldiers who could join him and greet the stranger at the gate. When the three of them stood in front of the heavy door, Madison gave the silent signal for the other two men to open it.

A being that resembled a man stood before them, but he looked more like a snow-covered hairy animal with the layers of animal pelts wrapped around him. When the man pulled down one of the pelts from his face, Madison gasped.

"Tehonawaga!"

The three of them jumped into action and ushered the Iroquois scout inside the fort. He pulled a travois behind him with a rope harness secured to his shoulders and waist. When Madison looked closer at the man, he realized it wasn't an animal fur on his back but the dead carcass of a deer. Five more were buried beneath pelts on the travois.

Once the Iroquois had been relieved of his heavy load, Madison placed his hands on Tehonawaga's upper arms and looked him straight in the eyes.

"Why have you come to the fort in this weather?"

"This is big day of celebration for you. I bring many deer. Everyone can eat and be full."

The response was delivered in such a logical manner, Madison had no rebuttal. It would be an insult to turn away such a gift, and they could use the meat. This man had risked his life to bring the special meal to the fort. Once the colonel learned of the offering, he would agree that they should all partake of it

Madison led the way to the main hall. He could well imagine the reaction from his fellow soldiers when they saw the bounty that had been provided for them. Although many of them from the northern colonies didn't often recognize the festivities surrounding this time because of the teachings of their church, those from the middle colonies did. Madison knew enough about it from his cousin's family, and it seemed like just what they all needed. It looked like Christmas this year would be a day to remember after all.

❧

"Divinia, come help Garrick put some sprigs of holly on the windowpanes." Mama held out the basket with the red-berried plants and waited for her two youngest to do as she asked. "Do not forget to secure them with the wax." She turned to her two middle sons. "Jerel and Kare, fetch the pomander balls from the vegetable cellar so we can attach the ribbons for hanging."

Pomander balls. Elanna closed her eyes and brought to mind the unique smells of citrus, cloves, and other spices. This year, Divinia and Garrick were allowed to use the nails to poke holes into the oranges. Elanna and Mama still oversaw the blending of the cinnamon, nutmeg, and orrisroot that went into those holes, but the younger children enjoyed being able to push the whole cloves into the skin of the oranges. Because the citrus fruit had to harden and cure, Elanna knew when they began, Christmas was just a few weeks away.

The smells of Christmas always brought a festive feel to the air. Just the other day, Elanna had combined rose petals, dried lavender, rosemary, and bayberry, then divided the fragrant mixture into netting tied with string to provide a pleasant holiday scent. The gray skies of winter might attempt to dampen her mood, but celebrating for twelve nights still brought her joy and hope amid the gloom.

Elanna sat in the rocking chair near the parlor fireplace. With each click of her knitting needles, muffs for Mama, Divinia, and herself took shape. Papa, Edric, Jerel, Kare, and Garrick would all receive scarves. The knitting used to fall on Mama's shoulders, but this year, Elanna had assumed the task. The coldest part of winter had yet to arrive, and she wanted her family to have new hand and face warmers when it did.

As she rocked and knitted, her mind wandered to the northern boundary of New York Colony and the fort where Madison was spending the winter. She could only imagine what type of shelter the fort provided with its stone walls and floors and drafty corridors. From what Madison wrote in his last letter, not an ounce of comfort existed for any of the soldiers. Although he assured her that the officers had straw ticks on their rope beds, the lack of a cozy room shared with loved ones around made even the least luxury seem like the barest of essentials.

Winters near New Castle most often saw only a handful of snowstorms, but the bitter cold, wet air could chill to the bone. Mama often heated bricks in front of the fireplace, then wrapped them in cloth and placed them at the foot of their beds before they retired for the night. Elanna sometimes used her brick to warm her hands instead of her feet. Madison wouldn't even have that to help him stay warm. But from what Mr. Witherspoon had told her, they had other resources. Madison could use stones instead, and he mentioned bearskins in his letter, which seemed like an excellent way to stay warm as long as one could get a sufficient supply of them. Frowning down at her knitting, she struggled to remember everything he had written in his letter dated November 25:

We saw the first snowflakes two days past. Although I do not wish to admit it, I know that winter will soon be upon us. Boston during the winter is quite cold, but out here in the middle of the wilderness without the protection of a snug home or structure, I fear it will be more brutal than any I have so far encountered. Thankfully, Tehonawaga and his

warriors have provided us with piles of bearskins and other
pelts, and we have all been chopping wood for the fireplaces,
praying it is enough to last.

Elanna still had trouble believing that the soldiers worked
side by side with the Indians in the wilderness. There
were several tribes south of where she lived, but they had
long been accustomed to the colonial settlements. Out in
the wilderness, life was surely much different. Did they
even engage in any Twelfth Night celebrations? The little
preparations she and her family made weren't much, but they
managed to make the time together special. Madison had no
family or loved ones with him—only the bitter cold and his
fellow soldiers to keep him company.

Oh, how she wished a letter would reach him, but Mr.
Witherspoon told her the snow fell much earlier up there
and with greater frequency. It made many of the roads
impassable and shut off contact with those at any distance
from the villages and towns. Well, Elanna might not be able
to reach him now, but she could at least make certain a letter
made its way to him as soon as the roads cleared enough for
a courier to deliver it.

Setting aside her needles, Elanna left everyone to their
individual tasks and slipped upstairs to the room she shared
with her sister, above the kitchen. It had been Mama's room
before her parents' deaths. Afterward, Mama had moved into
their room. When Elanna and Edric were born, Mama and
Papa had added the second section to the house. Now, they
had two complete staircases leading to the second story with
plans to expand further in a few more seasons. Despite the
meager beginnings Mama and Papa had when they married,
their farm was now thriving.

Elanna pulled out the chair in front of her desk with

its many compartments and drawers. Papa and two of his brothers had even added a couple secret sections behind two of the drawers where she could hide some of her treasured possessions. She reached into one now to pull out Madison's last letter. After reading it one more time—despite having most of it committed to memory—Elanna retrieved a sheet of paper and removed the lid from the inkwell.

With quill pen in hand, she started writing:

23 December 1756
Dear Major Clark,

I know this letter will not reach you until the spring thaw has come and the roads leading to the fort have become passable. But upon receipt of your last missive, I could do nothing until I penned a reply. Reading about the impending winter that will from all accounts see you buried under several feet of snow, I felt a chill sweep over me. You might be more familiar with how cruel winter can be from your years living in Boston, but I pray you fare well through this one, too.

We have begun preparations for our Twelfth Night festivities. The dried flowers are set out throughout the house, the pomander balls have been cured and hung, and the holly has been attached with wax to the windowsills. Before long, Mama will call for me to come downstairs so I can help her bake the gingerbread cookies and boil the wassail. If the skies continue to remain clear of snow, we might even take the wagon into town and serenade some of our fellow colonists with a few carols. When the cold keeps us inside, we sit in front of a blazing fire with warm cups of tea or wassail and listen to Papa read from the Bible or Mama share one of her stories from when she was a little girl. How I wish I could share this joyous season with you in more ways than through a poor description in a letter!

Did your family celebrate Twelfth Night? What did you do in Boston to help pass the long, gloomy days of winter? And how are you enduring the winter at the fort? I have been told that there will be no further fighting until warm weather returns, and for that I am most thankful. I long to know more about where you are staying, but only share what you are allowed to write. It would be unbearable to me if I learned some ill had befallen you because one of our letters had been intercepted and important details used to your harm.

I hear Mama calling from the kitchen. It is time for me to conclude. I pray often for your good health and well-being and that this winter passes quickly. May God keep you safe until you can write again. I anxiously await word that you are well.

Sincerely,
Miss Elanna Hanssen

After blotting the ink, Elanna set the letter aside and closed her desk. She would send the letter north at the earliest opportunity. Oh, how she prayed it would come soon.

six

Spring thaw arrived, and with it came the official reports from the war. It took a few weeks before the complete transition from winter to spring took place, but once it did, everything came alive—including the riders delivering the mail. Hearsay and murmurs had been heard throughout the valley. Some reports had the British pushing back the French into the Ohio Valley. Others told of the French closing in on the southeast area of New York. But until the facts appeared in the *Gazette*, many refused to believe them. Once they were in black and white, they couldn't be ignored.

Every year, Elanna loved to be outside among the new blooms and fields of green. The birds chirping and the animals coming out from hibernation always gave her an added zest for life. But this spring, concern for the colonists and the fate of the British filled her mind and thoughts. Benjamin, the courier, had left a couple weeks ago with her letter to Madison. She could only pray he was still alive to receive it.

"Elanna!" Mama called from the door off the kitchen. "We need to take all of the rugs outside and beat them free of dust. Then it's time to sweep the floors and rid the house of all the dirt that has accumulated during the winter."

She might wish for time to stand still, but planting season and cleaning waited for no one. At least she would have something to keep her mind focused away from Madison and the war—even if only for a little while. The windows needed to be washed, then opened to let in the fresh air. Papa and Edric had already gathered the farmhands together to begin plowing the fields and preparing the ground for planting. Jerel and Kare saw to the sheep, pigs, cows, and horses, while Garrett and Divinia tended to the chickens and geese.

"I am here, Mama," Elanna said as she approached the front door to their farmhouse.

Mama brushed a hand across her brow and paused to take several deep breaths. "I already removed the rugs from the kitchen and hallway, but there are still two more in the front room."

Elanna didn't like the way Mama looked. Her skin was flushed, and she appeared unsteady on her feet. She prayed Mama didn't have a fever.

"Mama, do not overburden yourself with this. I can beat the rugs. Sit down," she said gently, "and shave off pieces of lye for the water to wash the windows."

At other times, Mama would have protested, but not today. "Thank you, my dear," she said with a grateful look.

Elanna touched her mother's cheek and found it cool. "It is the least I can do." She gave Mama a gentle nudge in the direction of the bench at the kitchen table. "Now, please rest. I will come back inside when I finish, and we can begin the next item on the list."

The running of their farm took top priority over everything else. Although Elanna wanted more than anything to go into town and visit with Chelcy or learn how everyone had fared during the winter months, her assistance to Mama could not be replaced. She was just thankful she no longer had to avoid the pecking hens or shoo them from their nests to grab the eggs. That chore now belonged to Divinia.

The sooner Elanna started on what needed to be done, the sooner the day would come when they would take their butter and cheese into town to sell. Then she could have all of the information and visits with friends that she desired. For now, there was work to be done.

※

Hoofbeats pounded on the ground as two horses galloped down the lane to the house from the main road. Divinia had her hands in the soil of Mama's flower bed, clearing away the winter growth. Elanna paused from helping her sister and shielded her eyes from the sun as she tried to make out the identity of the two riders. Papa and Edric! They must have news from town. A meeting of the assembly had been called a few days ago.

When they reached the front of the house, they both hopped off before their horses came to a complete stop. Servants took the horses to the barn to be watered and fed. Divinia stood and ran to Papa, wrapping her arms around his waist.

"The two of you should not ride your horses so hard," Elanna chided. "You place both yourselves and them in danger."

Edric approached and draped his arm across her shoulders. "And you should not worry so much about us. I am beginning to think you and Mama have traded places."

Elanna swatted at her twin, but he ducked to avoid her assault.

"Will the two of you ever be tired of these games you play?" Papa asked as he walked with Divinia to the front door.

"No," they answered together, then laughed.

Papa shook his head and disappeared inside with their sister. No sooner had the door closed than Elanna whirled on Edric.

"So?"

"So what?" Edric gave her an innocent look.

"What took place at the meeting? Was it something important? Did you discuss any new developments?"

Edric held up his hands. "Slow down, Elanna. Put to me

one question at a time, and I might be inclined to tell you what you want to hear."

Her brother could be so difficult at times. If she didn't love him so much, she might not be so quick to agree to his requests. "Very well. What took place at the meeting?"

He lowered himself to the ground and stretched out his legs. Elanna joined him, her breath catching in her chest at what her brother might share.

"Do you recall last summer when Deputy Attorney General McKean came to speak at one of the assembly meetings?"

How could she forget? Madison had caught her eavesdropping outside the window. "Yes, the one where you made it possible for me to listen from the bushes."

"Correct. Since that day, he has been deeply involved with matters for the assembly and legislation both for our three lower counties and for Philadelphia." Edric picked a lone weed from along the edge of the flower bed lining the walkway and twirled the stem between his fingers. "It seems the assembly has been quite impressed with his leadership and his dedication, so they voted today to make him an active member."

Elanna straightened and widened her eyes. "Do you mean to say that Mr. McKean will now be attending the meetings?" From the moment she saw the distinguished gentleman, she had a feeling he would play a big role in future political events.

"He will attend when he is able, yes. He does have duties farther south in the county where he lives, but he has vowed to do everything he can to be present as often as possible."

"How exciting!" Elanna clapped her hands. "Perhaps he will replace the speaker who leads the meetings now. At least then, you would not have to worry about falling asleep."

"This is true," Edric agreed with a chuckle.

"So, did anything else happen at the meeting? News or developments?"

Her brother's expression changed, and worry crossed his features as he stared across their land. Elanna touched his arm.

"Edric, what is it?"

"I am afraid the news of the war is not good. You have heard about both the British and our provincial militia suffering heavy losses."

Elanna nodded, her stomach muscles tightening.

"The numbers are difficult to tally, but the French have advanced farther than anyone thought they might. Several forts have fallen into their hands, and the barbarous actions of both the Indians and the French that were reported in the papers last year are only growing worse."

Oh, Madison! Elanna's heart cried out for him. She had no way of knowing if his fort had been taken, or if he was anywhere near the sites of these battles.

"How will this affect us here?"

"That was the other topic discussed—at times in a heated manner—at the meeting this morning," Edric responded, weariness in his voice. "Papa told me there will be a meeting here next week to discuss how we can protect New Castle from possible French infiltration."

"A meeting here? At the house?"

"Yes."

Good. At least she wouldn't have to hide in the bushes this time. But she had to make sure Mama allowed her to serve the tea.

"What options do we have in case of attack?"

"I am not privy to everything that may be proposed. I only know what Papa has told me and what I have heard from the other men." He gave her a sideways grin. "You will find out soon enough. I am certain you will find a way to be present during the meeting."

Elanna nudged Edric with her shoulder, and he nudged

her back. The solid form of his body took her by surprise, pleasing and saddening her at the same time. With them both fast approaching their sixteenth birthday, their sometimes playful camaraderie would increasingly be replaced with a relationship constrained by adult responsibilities. He would take his place in the assembly and follow in Papa's footsteps, and she would marry and start a family of her own.

Marriage. Elanna sighed. Right now, Madison was the only prospect. . .and he was hundreds of miles away.

⁊⁊

"We must protect our town and every vested interest we have in it."

"What about our children and our wives? They must be our first priority in case of attack."

"And what about the cost of supplies? "

Elanna could hear the angry voices of the assembly members all the way in the kitchen, through two closed doors. She set out the tin cups and impatiently waited for the tea to boil. Mama had agreed to her request easily with the comment that their servant girl would appreciate the reprieve from serving tea. The opportunity allowed Elanna to freely observe everything that happened and to hear every detail of the discussion.

As she approached the sitting room, carrying her tray of now-steeping tea and cups, the voice of Thomas McKean traveled through the door.

"Gentlemen, we must keep our wits about us and remember that our fellow colonists will be looking to us to ease their troubled minds. They will want us to provide them with rational answers to their questions. They will look to us for leadership. We cannot allow our emotions to overtake our logical guidance."

Soft murmurs followed Mr. McKean's admonition, so Elanna took that moment to slip into the room, unobserved.

Remaining as inconspicuous as possible, she placed the tea tray on the table near the door, set out the refreshments, and slipped back outside. She had already brought her quilting supplies down, so she took a seat on the bench in the hall and resumed work on her latest piece.

"What do you suggest?"

Elanna wished she knew the men well enough to associate names with voices. Frowning in concentration, she completed her work by rote, keeping her focus on the meeting.

"We must first analyze the seriousness of the threat we face." Mr. McKean's voice was too distinctive to miss. "There is little chance that the French army will travel this far south, especially since the engagements to the north are keeping them quite occupied."

"Do you believe their navy will attempt attack by sea?" This came from Papa.

"That is exactly how I fear they might come," Mr. McKean affirmed. "Because many of our militia along with the British soldiers are occupied in the Ohio Valley, it is only logical that the French would send ships across the ocean to infiltrate our towns and ports along the shore."

"But we have no navy to withstand such an attack. The only vessels we have available are merchant ships full of goods."

"That is correct." Elanna could hear Mr. McKean's boots click on the hardwood floor, the sound increasing and receding as he paced. "And merchantmen are equipped and ready to defend themselves against any attack while at sea. Gentlemen, I propose we use every resource to our advantage. It would be possible to recruit marine merchants to station aboard every ship in the harbor. . . ."

As Mr. McKean launched into the plan of defense, Elanna's mind dwelled on the harsh reality they faced because of this war. Before, she had felt isolated and distant from everything Madison was experiencing. Now, however, she could taste the fear he must face every day. While he fought the French from one side, the men here would be fighting from the other. Together, they had to succeed. Mr. McKean's final words echoed this sentiment.

"We must do everything we can to keep the French out of the Delaware River. Our fellow colonists in Philadelphia are depending on us."

The meeting adjourned a moment later, so Elanna grabbed her basket and headed upstairs to her room. She had learned more than enough this evening to pen another letter to Madison.

❧

Another letter from Elanna. Each missive always made whatever calamity Madison had faced that day seem insignificant. He was glad he had been able to send his reply to her last letter right after the ice melted and the ground thawed. She should have received it by now. He had counted the days until the courier arrived, wanting to assure her that he was alive and well—even if he felt as if certain parts of his body would never feel warmth again. Although she filled the winter letter with descriptions of Christmas and celebrations, he could tell she was worried about him.

As he read this one, that concern switched sides. Ever since he had arrived at the fort to accept his command, he had secretly felt as if each success in battle contributed to Elanna's protection. He hadn't considered the threat that loomed from the ocean and the rivers. He tried to take comfort in the thought that she lived in an area governed by a strong assembly, in close proximity to Philadelphia, where more support could be counted on if needed.

"Major Scott?"

Matthew Lewis approached from the steps leading to the ramparts.

"Lieutenant," Madison acknowledged, then saw the bandage on his arm. "What happened?"

"This?" He waved a hand as though the wound were inconsequential. "It is nothing. An arrow nicked me yesterday. Bled a bit, but the doc tells me it is nothing more than a surface wound."

Madison didn't like seeing his men injured. He prided himself on being able to lead his men into battle and out of it, but during war, loss and injury were inevitable.

Matthew nodded at the letter in Madison's hands. "Another letter from your lady friend back home?"

"Not exactly home for me, but yes."

"But I thought you joined us from there."

"I did, but I came from visiting with my cousin's family in New Castle. My home is in Boston."

The lieutenant placed one hand on top of the other and rested them on the hilt of his sword. "But I never hear you speaking of Boston. It is always the young lady and the lower counties of Pennsylvania."

Madison ignored the knowing grin on his friend's lips. "Was there a reason you came to see me, Lieutenant?"

Matthew shrugged. "Only to inform you that the fields to the west are clear. No sign of enemy tribes or regiments."

"Considering how often the French have been attacking the other forts farther downriver, that news comes as quite a relief."

"Now, I suggest that we take a walk around the ramparts and you tell me about this latest letter."

With a one-day reprieve from the fighting, Madison welcomed the opportunity to share the thoughts that had been filling his mind of late.

"Lead the way."

He followed the lieutenant up the stone steps to the top of the fort. The wind whipped across the parapets, bringing cold air from the lakes to the west. Winter still clung stubbornly to this wild frontier, but in the end, spring would win. Madison couldn't wait to see what this land looked like clothed in green, with flowers dotting the ground and trees covered with delicate buds. Blue skies replacing the dismal gray would be a welcome sight. And game for hunting would once again be plentiful, so he and his fellow compatriots wouldn't have to survive on the barest essentials.

"Will I be forced to extract details from this letter, or will you share with me willingly?"

Madison shook his head and focused again on the lieutenant. "Do forgive me, Matthew. My mind became absorbed with imagining this land in full bloom."

"A natural reaction for any man, following a bitter winter such as we have just endured."

"Nevertheless, you asked for details. I am afraid there is not much I can share, as Miss Hanssen kept her missive quite short this time. She did, however, share about the increasing industry along the river south of Philadelphia."

"Industry of what kind?"

Madison stopped, shifted his sword, and leaned against the wall. "At present, there is a rather substantial shipbuilding outfit that is forging ships with iron and developing them into seaworthy vessels."

"I would never have thought any town south of Philadelphia would have the necessary fortifications in order to provide an industry such as that with support." Matthew leaned against the wall opposite Madison and pursed his lips. "It appears those three little counties are forming a colony of their own."

Madison nodded. "That thought did occur to me. They petitioned many years prior for a separate assembly in their own jurisdiction. With the recent increase in development and the pivotal location of those counties, it would not come as a surprise to me if they desire to govern themselves, as well."

"And what will you do if that happens?"

"I do not see how that decision affects mine in any way. My thoughts centered primarily on a trade once my time with the military has come to an end."

Matthew folded his arms. "I have often wondered the same myself."

"Although I never served as an apprentice, I have always had a skill with iron."

The lieutenant seemed to follow his lead. "And with the shipbuilding growing every day. . . "

"Exactly. There would be great opportunity to get involved at the onset of the industry rather than once it is already established."

"It appears to me you have the entire matter settled in your mind." Matthew spread his arms wide and grinned. "You did not even need my advice."

"Yes." Madison chuckled. "But it is always good to receive affirmation from a friend."

The lieutenant stood erect, his shoulders back, as if about to assume an important role. "In that case, I believe you are quite astute to consider a trade once your service in the military is complete. And moving closer to your lady friend makes that decision all the more worthwhile." He relaxed. "There. Now you have my advice."

Madison stepped forward and clapped the man on his shoulder. "I am a fortunate man to have you serving beside me here, Matthew."

The lieutenant mirrored Madison's stance. "And I am fortunate to serve under your command, sir."

"Now that our mutual gratitude is behind us, let us adjourn to the main hall for some sustenance. I do not know about you, but I am famished."

Matthew saluted. "As you command, sir. My stomach will be grateful."

As they climbed down from the ramparts, plans for the future and the excitement of joining the shipbuilding industry filled Madison's head. If only the war didn't hinder him from moving forward with those plans. He prayed they would see an end soon—and that it would be a favorable one for the colonies.

seven

Elanna walked up and down the rows of mounds in the western field. The farmhands had everything under control, but she still enjoyed surveying the progress of their crops.

"Everythin' all right, Miss Elanna?"

"I beg your pardon?" She turned toward the gravelly voice to find one of the workers wiping his brow with a dirty handkerchief.

"I was wonderin' if you found a problem with the plantin', the way you be lookin' at the rows, there."

"Oh, no. Everything is fine, Samson." This was one of the workers she knew by name. "I merely enjoy walking among the crops and—"

"Seein' how far they come?" he supplied.

"Yes!" She beamed. "How did you know?"

Samson chuckled. "I do the same thing, Miss Elanna. It makes a man proud to see what he has accomplished."

Elanna didn't often spend a long period of time in the fields, so she didn't have a relationship with any of the workers. She felt a kinship with Samson, though. He put a lot of effort into his work and took great pride in a job well done. That showed by the production levels the farm reached each season.

"Yes, it does, Samson. My family is fortunate to have you working with us."

He mopped his face again and dipped his head. "It be my pleasure, Miss Elanna. Your family has a good farm, here. I am glad your papa saw fit to hire me." He looked off to the south. "Now, I best be gettin' back to work."

"Of course, Samson. I do apologize if I have kept you."

"I was right happy to talk with you."

Elanna watched Samson walk toward the south fields, his stride confident. Pleasure filled her that the work her family gave him allowed him to walk tall. Some of the neighboring farms didn't have that benefit. She had heard stories of disgruntled workers and proprietors who actually beat their farmhands and slaves for not working hard enough. The mere idea of that sent shudders up Elanna's back. How one man could beat or attack another, she didn't know.

Just like the war.

Madison faced that kind of brutality almost every day—men attacking other men for what they felt was their right. But where would it all lead?

She wanted more answers, and she knew just where to get them.

Tempted to grab hold of her petticoats and run back to the house, Elanna looked around to find far too many people milling about. Someone would spot her, and when Mama found out. . . No, she didn't want to be on the receiving end of that scolding. She would walk.

"Mama!" she called as she pushed open the door to the kitchen and stepped inside.

"In here, Elanna," Mama replied.

Her voice sounded like it came from the sitting room, so Elanna headed in that direction. She stepped up into the hallway and rounded the corner near the front of the house to find Mama weaving with Divinia.

"What are you making?"

"A potholder," Divinia answered without looking up. She kept her focus on her work. The little wool square with the warp threads secured to the loom had already taken shape. As Divinia worked, her tongue peeked out one corner of her mouth.

Elanna almost laughed at the sight but held back. It wasn't too long ago that she had sat in the same chair where Divinia did now.

"Was there something you needed?"

She shifted her gaze to Mama and nodded. "Yes. I would like to spend a little time in Wilmington." Should she also share the reason for wanting to go? "And I wish to pay a visit to Mr. Witherspoon as well."

Mama's eyebrows rose at this. "Without a chaperone?"

"No, I thought Edric might be able to accompany me. He said this morning that he needed some additional grain for the second harvest. We could stop by the granary on our way home."

"Hmm." Mama pursed her lips and resumed her weaving for several moments.

Only the sound of the two pieces of wool thread brushing against each other filled the room. Elanna waited, but she shifted from one foot to the other.

"Very well," Mama finally said. "Go find Edric and ask him if he can get away from the fields in order to take you."

Elanna started to leave, but Mama's voice stopped her.

"I expect you to also purchase some supplies for me in New Castle on your way back home."

"Yes, Mama," Elanna replied.

After writing down the items Mama needed, she went to find her brother.

৯

Edric pulled the wagon to a halt in front of the journalist's office and set the brake.

Elanna stood and placed a hand on the back of the seat, but Edric jumped down and rushed to her side to assist. Placing her hands on his shoulders, she allowed him to help her to the ground, then looked up at him.

"I am glad you are coming inside with me. You will no doubt find the topics of our conversation interesting with your future place in the assembly."

Edric quirked an eyebrow. "You will be discussing the war, I presume?"

"Yes, as well as some of Mr. Witherspoon's experiences as a journalist. As you may recall, when last we met, he regaled me with details of covering a story in Williamsburg when Colonel Washington returned from the Ohio Valley."

He touched two fingers to his chin. "I believe I will enjoy another visit." Extending his arm, he turned toward the building. "Shall we?"

Elanna placed her hand in the crook of his arm and walked with him up the steps to the door. After being admitted by the servant and their presence announced, they waited for Mr. Witherspoon. The journalist appeared almost immediately.

"Miss Hanssen. A pleasure to see you again." He approached with a smile as his gaze took in Edric as well, but a flash of disappointment appeared on his face. "And I see your brother has also accompanied you."

Perhaps he was not happy that she had brought a chaperone? But it wouldn't be proper otherwise. "Edric is a clerk to the assembly in New Castle and plans to join them upon attaining eighteen years."

Witherspoon's expression changed to one of approval. "An admirable pursuit, Mr. Hanssen. I have had many dealings with various members of the assembly, both here and in Philadelphia. I applaud your choice of professions."

Edric seemed flattered. "Thank you. I am sure it will remain a significant power in regard to the political issues we face every day."

"Of that, I have no doubt," the journalist agreed. "Already, members have advocated on behalf of the colonists in retaliation of British laws enforced upon the eight royal colonies. The three proprietary colonies, with private landowner governance, hold a high level of appreciation for the assembly. Much like the two charter colonies of Rhode Island and Connecticut with settlers running the administration."

"Our father often says that the assembly can bring about great change through our influence and decisions."

"And with that influence comes great responsibility. It is imperative that the members understand their position and the faith and trust the colonists place in them."

Elanna waited for the two to pause in their exchange, so as not to appear discourteous. "Will it meet with your agreement if Edric joins us this afternoon?"

The journalist turned toward her, almost as if he had forgotten she also stood with Edric.

"Of course! Please, come with me." Mr. Witherspoon led the way down the hall to the back of the building and his private office. "We shall continue our discussion in my office."

Like all the other times, Elanna found it amazing that the journalist managed to keep such a tidy workspace. From the polished mahogany desk with minimal paper on top to the shelves free of dust and the chandelier above without any sign of cobwebs.

"Are you certain travel takes up the majority of your work?"

She looked at Edric as he asked the question but saw Mr. Witherspoon pause and regard her brother with a puzzled expression.

"Yes, why do you ask?"

"This area is so clean. Either you spend an infrequent amount of time here, or—"

"Or I cannot abide writing in an unkempt space," he finished for Edric. "It distracts me from my focus and inhibits the free flow of my thoughts. The printing room is where the disarray remains," he said with a grin.

Mr. Witherspoon gestured toward the two Queen Anne chairs facing his desk. "Please, take a seat." Once they did, he continued. "Now, Miss Hanssen," the journalist addressed her. "Tell me what brings you to Wilmington this afternoon." He chuckled. "For I am certain it is more than the pleasure of my company."

Elanna found his sense of humor amusing. It reminded her of Madison, although the major's charm was much more appealing. At least Mr. Witherspoon made conversation enjoyable—unlike the speaker of the New Castle Assembly, whose droning voice lulled her to sleep.

"I read your last article where you mentioned a militia group by the name of Rogers' Rangers. They are fighting near Lake George, where Mad—" She caught herself. "Where Major Scott is posted."

Witherspoon templed his fingers and rested his elbows on his desk. "Ah, yes. This is your friend, the one you spoke about at our last meeting."

"Yes. I have received a couple letters from him, and he only mentioned the name Roger."

"I cannot see that he would state anything else. Information such as that found in a private letter could compromise the safety of the men fighting in the northern New York region, should the letter be intercepted."

Elanna drew her eyebrows together. "But you wrote about it in the paper. Can that not also put their safety at risk should someone in the French army read it?"

"You are quite astute," the journalist complimented, "but I merely made a reference to the militia. I did not provide any specific details that might betray their location or their fighting tactics."

"What are the unique fighting methods they use?" Maybe

Madison knew the rangers or had fought with them at some point.

"Unlike the regulars, who are trained in bold linear marches and firing formations, Rogers' Rangers employ tactics used by earlier European armies. Against the French and the Indians, who take to the hills and conceal themselves behind trees prior to their attacks, these methods prove to be quite useful." He leaned back in his chair and took a deep breath. "They have become the primary scouts for the British, and although their battle against the French ended without a decisive conclusion, their use of snowshoes on the snow-covered ground near Lake George gave them a distinct advantage."

"What are snowshoes?" Edric shifted to the edge of his chair.

"Broad shoes that distribute a man's weight in a way that prevents him from sinking into high drifts of snow. While the French floundered in snow up to their knees, the rangers maintained their positions on the high ground."

Elanna almost laughed at the image the journalist's words painted in her mind. She could imagine what Madison would look like in shoes like that and made a mental note to ask about them in her next letter.

"Nevertheless, the French outnumbered them, and had it not been for the setting of the sun, the casualties might have been far worse."

"How is it that you have come to be so informed, and in such great detail?"

"I have several couriers who carry information from the battle sites to me, and I retrieve what I need from other reports or from the mouths of the colonists and militia who have lived the stories about which I write."

She counted herself fortunate to have met Mr. Wither-spoon. Waiting for word from Madison had proven to be difficult at best, but thanks to the added details from the journalist, Elanna could fill in the holes and appease her curiosity.

"Shall I show you some of what I have collected thus far on the war?"

Oh, that would be perfect. "Yes, please," she said.

Edric also seemed delighted at the prospect of learning more about the battles taking place farther north. His quiet observance made Elanna wish she had inherited that trait rather than her insatiable thirst for knowledge. But as Mr. Witherspoon presented article after article, she decided her traits suited her just fine.

❧

Madison knelt in front of the river and cupped his hands, then plunged them into the flowing currents of the Hudson. Without giving it a second thought, he dumped the cool water over his head. The rivulets ran down his face and neck and seeped into the fabric of his shirt. Relief from the oppressive humidity followed. In early April, they had been buried in snow drifts taller than they. Now, in the fourth week of August, they were begging for a reprieve from the heat.

He leaned over the water and stared at his distorted reflection. Images from the recent battle at Fort William Henry flashed through his mind. The faces of the massacred soldiers—even women and children—floated in front of him in succession. It had been a brutal siege, and their militia, along with the British 35th Regiment, had resisted for several days.

Madison had followed Lieutenant Colonel Monro's lead, and their men had fought with valor. But it wasn't enough. Montcalm's army overpowered them. Madison could still see the look on Monro's face when the message from General Daniel Webb revealed that reinforcements wouldn't be coming. Such defeat should never have been seen on any man. Monro had no choice but to surrender. Thankfully, Montcalm agreed to allow them to leave with their weapons and retreat without being attacked.

If only the escort to Fort Edward by Montcalm and his army had worked. But the French-allied Indians had discovered their early morning departure and attacked the column. Madison didn't recall much of what happened in the panic that ensued. Over two thousand soldiers and civilians, and three hundred of them never made it to Fort Edward.

Madison clenched his fists as he rocked back on his heels and looked to the sky. "Why God? Why do You allow such atrocities? You could have stopped it, but You didn't. How could You let those innocent women and children die like that?"

He tried to erase the fear and horror on those faces from his mind, but it was no use. One little girl in particular haunted him day and night. She could have been Elanna as a child. The resemblance was uncanny, right down to the upturned nose and round face. He prayed the little girl would be spared a horrifying fate.

"Major Scott?"

Madison looked up to find Benjamin standing next to him with a letter in his hand.

"I have another letter from your Miss Hanssen, sir. Lieutenant Lewis said I would find you here."

Madison stared at the missive. It was as if thoughts of her alone had conjured up the courier and brought the message to him. He took the letter.

"Thank you, Benjamin." He glanced to the north, up the Hudson toward where he knew Fort William Henry now lay in ruins. "Did you encounter much difficulty reaching us?"

"Do you mean in regard to the siege and massacre up river?"

He turned back toward Benjamin. "Yes. I had wondered how long it would be before we would see anyone from the outside."

Benjamin shrugged. "I have had more challenging days."

"Well, I will not detain you any further. You no doubt have more missives to deliver." Madison reached into his pouch and withdrew the letter he'd written last night. It detailed as much as he could share about the horrors of the siege. He placed it with the letter to Philadelphia. "Please see that these are delivered as soon as possible."

Benjamin took the post and slipped it into his own pouch. "I shall guard them with my life, sir."

Madison nodded his thanks. "Now, you should not tarry much longer." He grinned and gestured toward the mail pouch. "There might even be a letter from a special lady for another soldier in there."

The courier chuckled. "Perhaps." He saluted. "It is good to see you still alive, sir."

"It is good to still be alive, Benjamin."

As soon as the courier left, Madison held Elanna's missive in his hands and stared at it. Unable to resist, he broke the seal and unfolded the parchment. Her familiar scrawl warmed his heart.

My dear Major Scott, it began.

The personal address preceding his name gave him pause. He didn't want to read too much into it, but his mind raced with possibilities. Where had her thoughts been when she sat down to write to him? What happened to set her mind on such a personal path? Was she implying something more than friendship existed between them?

Writing on June 13, Elanna began with talk about the first harvest and the bounty they had reaped from the early planting. He could almost taste the fresh fruits and vegetables and smell the canned preserves as they stored them away in jars for the fall and winter months. How he wished he could be there to share those moments with her. But the third paragraph caught his eye.

Edric escorted me into Wilmington today, where I again met with Mr. Witherspoon, the journalist I mentioned in previous correspondence. He shared so many new and fascinating reports from his travels to Boston, New York, Philadelphia, and Williamsburg. His work takes him to so many places, and he has the good fortune to witness exciting events as they are happening. Rather than read about them afterward, he lives them and writes about them. I find my time spent with him is much more productive than all the occasions when I eavesdropped on assembly meetings.

Madison grinned at this and recalled when he had discovered her doing exactly that. Their time together immediately following still held a special place in his heart. He regretted not being able to remain with her longer than that day, and hearing about her visits with the journalist only heightened that remorse. It should be he supplying her with the information and knowledge she sought, not this Mr. Witherspoon.

He has numerous stories to share, and as long as I am able to persuade Mama to permit my visits with him, I will continue to absorb all that he will impart to me.

"Stories better be all that he imparts," Madison muttered, then caught himself as he realized how jealous that sounded. It wouldn't do him any good to dwell on those feelings now, not when he was too far away to do anything about them.

He finished reading and learned that Elanna had celebrated her sixteenth birthday in July. Once again, guilt surfaced. He vowed to make it up to her when he saw her again and prayed he would have that chance.

As he folded her letter, he noticed another piece of paper underneath. It was torn from the *Gazette* in Boston. One word stood out above all the rest.

Smallpox.

He scanned the contents of the brief article. The tribes who had attacked the helpless colonists at Fort William Henry had also disinterred, scalped, and robbed from the fort's cemetery. But smallpox had clung to the bodies buried there. A devastating outbreak of the illness had swept through the Indian encampments. They had carried the disease back with them on the bodies of the dead, and the majority of them had died as a result.

" 'Whatsoever a man soweth, that shall he also reap,' " Madison quoted. "They received the punishment that was due them." A pang of remorse hit, but he ignored it.

"Lord, I should be saddened by any loss of life. I know Thou doest not rejoice when a soul is lost forever. But I cannot feel regret." He sighed. "I should have remained and fired upon as many as I could with my rifle, rather than fleeing for my own life and watching others die. It is good to know that Thou didst claim the vengeance, as Thou hast promised. At least those victims did not die in vain."

But that still didn't eliminate the sense of vindication he felt. A part of him wished he had been present to deliver the justice. The other part of him wished for it all to end. He was tired of the killing, the blood, and the innocent suffering.

eight

Madison walked around the perimeter of Fort Edward and rubbed his hands on his upper arms to ward off the chill in the air. Temperatures were dropping once again, and that meant yet another cold winter buried beneath layers of animal pelts with nothing to warm him but thoughts of Elanna. He paused on the west side of the fort and looked across the Hudson at the barracks, officer's house, and military hospital on the island in the center of the river. Many of the captives from that summer's massacre had been treated there for their wounds, and a quarantine area had been reserved for the smallpox sufferers.

He still couldn't believe such a great number managed to escape not only their Indian captors but also the smallpox. The good Lord had certainly shone His favor on them this time.

"After all that has happened this year, it is difficult to believe that we remain a stronghold at this fort."

Madison turned at the voice. "Captain Rogers." At Rogers's salute, he responded in kind. "And yes, it is."

"What draw is there that brings you to the riverbanks?"

He jerked his chin over his shoulder at the fort. "The confines in there had become rather stifling. When I begin to feel more like a slave in the hold of a ship than an officer, it is time for a breath of fresh air."

Rogers nodded. "I know exactly what you mean. The training of my rangers on the island gives me a reprieve from the close quarters we are forced to endure inside those walls."

"At least you have barracks and ranger huts to offer shelter away from the other regiments."

"And do not forget the officer's house I had constructed last month," Rogers pointed out.

"How could I forget?" Madison cleared his throat. "You are now the envy of almost every officer posted here."

The military trainer shrugged. "Can I help it if my work requires long hours on the island? We often train well after nightfall and rise the next day before the sun. It was a requisition of necessity."

"And of comfort," Madison parried.

Rogers opened his mouth as if to deny it but grinned instead. "I plead guilty as charged."

"As well you should." Madison placed one hand on Rogers's shoulder and with the other, pointed an index finger at him. "Do not forget, I have observed your training procedures and exercises. I am well aware of the added measures you take to provide you and your rangers with a suitable reward following a successful training exercise."

"Can you find fault with my actions?"

"Not a one."

Rogers reached into his pouch and pulled out a piece of parchment with a list written on it. "Lord Loudon will feel the same, I pray, when he receives the letter I posted just last month."

"The simpleton commander-in-chief of the English forces?" Madison had met him once in England before he crossed the ocean to Boston. How the man had ever been placed in a position of authority and leadership was beyond him.

"The very same," Rogers replied. "My American rangers have little regard for him or his lack of military prowess. Had they been present during the escapade at Louisburg, I have no doubt the results would have been quite different."

"Had the outcome been different there, we might still be in possession of Fort William Henry."

"This is true." Rogers sighed. "Instead, we lose a good fort to the French and must flee for our lives while Loudon retreats to Long Island and sets up camp there."

"What was included in your letter?"

Rogers held out the piece of parchment. Madison, taking it, read the words *Ranging Rules* at the top.

"I have detailed my method of training and rules of order, which differ from the way the British confront their enemy on the battlefield."

"So rather than the long lines of military advance, you're proposing a return to the older forms of warfare where we make use of our surroundings and take our enemy by surprise attack—just like the Indians and French utilizing the cover of trees or hills."

"Only without the savagery and disrespect for their fellow humans."

Madison had seen these tactics in action, and they led to greater success than British methods. He handed the paper back to Rogers.

"I pray these lords and governors find merit in my methods and begin to employ them with their own armies. I would be more than willing to establish a training ground here at the fort and increase the number of rangers tenfold."

"That would certainly put us at an advantage over our enemy during this war." Madison's own regiment had been able to withstand a greater onslaught, and fight with fewer casualties as a result of Rogers's training. "I have no doubt we would see the tides turn in our favor."

"We can only hope."

❧

November disappeared into December as the blustery winds

once again blew across the scenic landscape surrounding the Hudson River. Christmas came and went, and the new year along with it. Madison reflected on the battles he and his fellow colonists had fought. The war had been raging for four years, but only two since England had sent assistance to their cause. He could see the growing disillusionment in his regiment and in his fellow officers. The dismal and bitter cold winter didn't help matters.

Madison walked away from the north barracks, following a meeting of the commanding officers. Plans existed for a midwinter strike on Fort Carillon and St. Frederick near Lake Champlain. As Lord Loudon mounted his attack plan, the forces at Fort Edward were to remain at their posts, awaiting further orders. With the freezing temperatures and the limited rations, Madison didn't know how successful an attack would be. And if the snowstorms continued, the ability to leave the fort would be eliminated. They had already lost several men to frostbite and others who froze to death.

"Major Scott!"

Madison halted at the frantic voice of a captain approaching from the corridor.

"Lieutenant Lewis, sir," the captain managed through labored breaths, bracing his hands on his knees.

"Take your time, Randolph."

"The lieutenant. He has wandered outside of the fort. No one has heard from him for a while, sir. They fear he might be lost in the snowstorm."

Not Matthew! Why would he have left the safety of the fort?

"How long has he been gone?"

Captain Randolph stood erect, finally able to breathe normally. "We are not certain, sir. We think perhaps two hours or more."

"Two hours? A man could die out there in that amount of time." Madison barely contained his anger, but he knew it wasn't the captain's fault. He closed his eyes and inhaled, forcing himself to remain calm. Anxiety wouldn't help Matthew. "All right. Go find Captain Rogers. Tell him to organize a search group. We will meet at the front gate, and I will issue further orders at that time."

"Yes, sir!" Randolph saluted then turned on his heels and left.

"Matthew, how could you wander away and not inform someone of your destination?" Madison muttered to himself. "I pray you found some form of shelter from these elements."

He reached his quarters in record time and threw together everything he might need for the trek into the storm. Lanterns were available in the magazine, so he raced to the main gate. Almost a quarter of his regiment and half of Rogers' Rangers awaited his arrival. He nodded his thanks to Rogers.

"Men, time is critical," he addressed the group. "We do not know in what condition we will find Lieutenant Lewis. But find him we shall. I will not return until we do."

"My men are in agreement with you, Major." Rogers stepped forward, his face full of regret. "We will do as you command."

Madison broke up the group into smaller teams and gave them orders to head out in each direction. He left two men behind to guide the teams back to the fort.

"Wait twenty-five minutes," he instructed the two soldiers. "If all of us have not returned, fire your muzzles in succession until we do."

He took Captain Randolph and Sergeant Davis with him and headed due north. The crunch of their footsteps in the snow provided a steady cadence to the whistle of the howling wind. With a lantern lighting the path ahead, Madison plunged into the powdery depths. He held a wool scarf in front of his mouth and nose and kept his arms close to his body. The frozen pellets mixed with the falling snow bit into the small area of exposed skin, like a thousand pinpricks centralized in one location.

"Lewis!" he hollered into the snowy abyss.

Randolph and Davis echoed him, but their yells seemed to get swallowed by the storm. They continued to yell as they plodded. Madison peered in front of him for any sign of tracks or evidence that Matthew might have come this way. Each step they took and each minute that passed was one more added to the time Matthew had been out in these conditions.

Every so often, he would peer back over his shoulder and make sure Randolph and Davis still followed him. They already had one man lost. They didn't need any more.

"Lord, please," he prayed to himself. "Thou knowest where he is. Guide my steps and the steps of these men to Lewis. We need Thy help."

He prayed Matthew had remembered his training and remained stationary the moment he realized he couldn't make it back to the fort. Otherwise, they might never find him.

A shot rang out into the night. One minute later, another followed. Twenty-five minutes had passed, and obviously everyone hadn't returned.

"Major Scott, we should turn around," Randolph suggested. "We do not know if Lieutenant Lewis came this way, or even if another team might have found him. If we stay out here any longer, we endanger our own lives."

The captain was right. Even now, Madison's fingers were numb, and he could barely feel his feet or legs. But he couldn't leave his friend alone out there. Randolph and Davis were also exposed to the bitter cold. They needed to get back to the fort, as well. Madison agreed to return, but if Lewis wasn't with any of the other men, he would venture out again—alone if necessary.

"Let us return," he ordered, unable to conceal the despair in his voice.

Randolph took the lantern and led the way. After five steps, Madison halted. The frozen Hudson lay to their right. Matthew had mentioned earlier needing to go to the island to see a soldier in the hospital who had been wounded several weeks ago. Surely he wouldn't have attempted that tonight.

"Not in weather like this," Madison muttered.

But try as he might, he couldn't move forward without at least taking a few steps in that direction. Davis noticed his slight veer to the right.

"Major Scott? Where are you going? The fort is south. You are headed west, toward the river."

Randolph stopped as well and raised the lantern high.

"I have a hunch," Madison informed them. "I promise we will not tarry long. But I must investigate this spot near the river."

The shots from the fort continued. They didn't have much time.

With careful steps and kicking into the drifts as far as the packed snow would allow him, Madison searched the area near where the three of them stood. Just as he was about to turn back to his team, he bumped into something solid. Peering into the dark with just a hint of the lantern piercing the blackness, Madison managed to make out the shape of a man, half buried in the snow. His breath caught in his throat.

"Lewis!"

He dug around the still form and tried to free him from the powdery prison. Praying for some sign of life, he leaned close to Lewis's mouth and offered up silent thanks when warm breath fluttered across his cheek. Randolph and Davis flanked him on both sides.

"He is alive!" Madison exclaimed. "Quick. We must get him back to the fort."

With Davis now holding the lantern, Madison and Randolph grabbed Lewis's arms and legs and turned toward Fort Edward. The shots' sounding led them to the front gate. A flurry of activity ensued as Lewis was taken to the infirmary area to be treated. When the weather cleared enough, they'd transport him to the island.

Once inside the nearest barracks, Madison tried to peel off his outer clothing. Without any feeling in his fingers, the task was impossible. Captain Rogers stood nearby and offered his assistance.

"We should get you to the infirmary, too," he declared as he peered at Madison's blue-tinged hands. "Those fingers look bad."

≈

"What have you heard about this?"

Elanna marched into Mr. Witherspoon's office with Edric trailing behind her just one day after the grounds had warmed enough to ensure safe travel. Winter had been mild, but temperatures had dropped well below freezing at times. With no word from Madison, she had only his most recent letter to keep her company.

"Miss Hanssen!" Mr. Witherspoon's wooden chair creaked as he stood, bracing his palms on the edge of his desk. "What a pleasant surprise, this is."

A momentary pang of embarrassment hit her at not taking the time to announce her arrival, but her desire to learn more about Madison superceded it. Her heart had ached with the pain she had read in his words about the massacre. She needed to know if any more information was at hand.

"I do apologize for my rather bold entrance, Mr. Witherspoon, but I must know." She held out the page of Madison's letter that mentioned the massacre at Fort William Henry. "What else have you heard about this event?"

Mr. Witherspoon took the page from her and perused it for several moments. He tapped his fingers to his lips and mumbled once or twice. Edric occupied the time by looking out the window and not paying either of them much attention. Elanna shifted her weight from one foot to the other and smoothed her hands down the sides of her petticoats. Finally, Mr. Witherspoon looked at her.

"This Major Scott," he began and gestured toward the letter. "How much do you know about him?"

The question surprised Elanna. "I have met him on two separate occasions and am well acquainted with his cousin and her family in New Castle." She tilted her head. "Why do you ask?"

He stepped away from his desk and faced the beveled glass window behind it. After an intake of breath, he slowly released it, his shoulders and back rising and falling with the action. His silence brought a small modicum of fear to Elanna's thoughts. Up until that day, she had been confident in Madison's honor. He had given her no reason to believe otherwise. But what did Mr. Witherspoon know?

The journalist faced her once more, his expression one of controlled indifference, yet a hint of concern remained evident.

"Perhaps you should take a seat." He extended his arm across his desk toward the two Queen Anne chairs opposite.

Elanna gathered her petticoats and sat, keeping her posture rigid. Edric joined her, remaining silent. Mr. Witherspoon took time to regard them both before he spoke but focused more on her. She felt her neck grow warm under his scrutiny. It almost seemed as if he weighed his words and considered how she might receive them. Not knowing what he was about to share with her, she had no choice but to wait.

"Miss Hanssen, before I provide you with additional information regarding the brutal attack your Major Scott has mentioned in his letter, I want to assure you that I mean no ill intent toward him or you."

Elanna nodded, trying hard to contain her impatience. "I appreciate that, Mr. Witherspoon."

He came around his desk and leaned back against it, clasping his hands in front of him. "You already know that I have a wealth of resources at my fingertips to gain news from both the battlefield and the local happenings."

She inclined her head.

"It is this intricate network of resources that affords me the opportunity to keep my finger on the pulse point of all that is taking place." Reaching behind him, he retrieved the page from Madison's letter and looked at it again. "You have shared some information about Major Scott during our visits, but I cannot help but assume there is more to your relationship."

Elanna averted her eyes at his statement.

"By your reaction, I can see that I am correct in that assumption." He lowered the page to his side and shifted his position. "Which is why I feel compelled to share this with you now."

She forced herself to once again meet his gaze. Her heart pounded inside her chest, and dampness formed on her palms. Keeping them enfolded in her petticoats, she waited for the journalist to continue.

"I know you are aware of the savagery and brutal treatment forced upon many of our fellow colonists by the French and the Indians against whom they fight."

"Yes," she managed to rasp out.

"In retaliation, reports of equal brutality on the side of the British and our militia have been brought back from the battlefields. Some have returned the heinous acts with vile encounters of their own."

He paused and moved to stand next to her. When he touched her arm, she started, and he withdrew his hand.

"Your Major Scott's name has been among those listed as performing such deeds."

No! That couldn't be true. Madison would never engage in such activities. His regard for others and his integrity, which seemed to be as much a part of him as breathing, would never allow him to commit such acts against another human being. Surely, she couldn't have been so mistaken about him.

The room seemed to spin as the journalist's words filtered through Elanna's mind. Dark spots appeared at the corners of her eyes, and she fought hard to maintain her composure. She refused to swoon. Clenching her fists tighter into her petticoats, she took several deep breaths to clear the haze around her vision and bring everything back into focus. Edric placed a hand on her arm, but it didn't bring much reassurance. Her heart still pounded, but she managed to swallow around the lump in her throat enough to respond.

"Mr. Witherspoon," she rasped. "Are you certain?"

Regret transformed his features. Elanna searched his eyes for any sign of duplicity or ill intent. She found none. Only concern and sorrow filled his gaze.

"How long has it been since you have received word from him?"

"Several months," she answered honestly, trying hard to keep the disappointment from her voice.

"And the last post you received included his report on the

massacre, yet nothing more has followed since?"

Elanna's shoulders fell with the weight of sadness at Madison's silence. "Yes," was all she could manage.

"Miss Hanssen, I truly wish I had not seen Major Scott's name anywhere other than to praise his efforts on behalf of the British during this war. As I stated earlier, I want only good tidings for you." He once again demonstrated his uneasiness through his tone and expression. "Because of that, you deserve to know the truth. I only regret that I am the one who must deliver it to you."

Elanna took note of Mr. Witherspoon's proximity then shifted her gaze to his face. In that moment, she observed his smooth brow, high cheekbones, and the aristocratic upturn of his nose. Light brown hair pulled back and tied in a precise pigtail only complemented the rest of his polished appearance. Not a hair was out of place. Not a wrinkle could be found on his pressed breeches or superbly tied cravat. He reminded her of Papa the one time they had traveled to Philadelphia to attend a gala in honor of the governor there.

She almost touched Mr. Witherspoon's hand but held back. A part of her longed to confide in someone, but she felt like she was betraying Madison in her thoughts. The other part wanted nothing more than to rush home and compose another letter to him. Whatever she decided, she needed to get away from here.

Elanna stood in haste, and Mr. Witherspoon stepped back. Edric quickly followed.

"I do apologize, but we must leave."

Anxiety appeared in Mr. Witherspoon's eyes, and he stayed her with a hand. "Will you come again to see me?"

"Right now, I am not certain." So many thoughts whirled inside her head. She couldn't keep them all straight.

"Miss Hanssen, please do not leave without the promise

that I will have the pleasure of your company again." His earnest gaze held her in place. "In the meantime, I shall do my best to uncover more details concerning Major Scott, that we might learn the truth behind the vague reports that have been brought to my attention."

His dedication and desire to put her mind at ease warmed her heart. Elanna couldn't in good conscience disregard that, so she offered him the briefest of nods. "Very well, Mr. Witherspoon. We shall return at the earliest convenience."

A partial grin formed on his lips, and he released a sigh. "Thank you, Miss Hanssen. I am most pleased." He raised her gloved hand to his lips and brushed a kiss across her knuckles.

"Good day, Mr. Witherspoon."

Elanna tried hard not to run from the room, but the feelings he evoked in her gave her reason to worry. Edric's presence helped keep her steps slow. Until today, Mr. Witherspoon had been a friend providing information and additional details to appease her curious mind. But now, she sensed a change in their relationship. Although not like the one she shared with Madison, it thrilled her just the same.

She needed time to make sense of the disturbing images brought on by Mr. Witherspoon's words concerning Madison. And she needed to make sure she didn't reveal any of this in her next letter to him.

nine

"It has finally happened!"

Madison looked up from writing to Elanna to see Lieutenant Matthew Lewis approach, waving a newspaper in his hand. After weeks of recovering from frostbite, Madison relished being able to hold the pen with his fingers. Now he enjoyed the chance for an afternoon outside in the fresh air, just outside the fort. The added space gave him the right amount of inspiration. It was already April 19, 1758—far too long since he'd sent a letter to Elanna.

"What has?" Madison asked as Matthew came to a stop in front of him.

"Lord Loudon. He has been recalled to England."

Thank the good Lord! Madison blotted the page where he had just written, then closed his journal. "I must say, it certainly took England long enough to realize how unfit he was to command all of the British armies here in the colonies."

Matthew took a seat next to Madison. "I second that!" He regarded the paper in his hand and scanned the article. "There is even a quote from Benjamin Franklin here about England's decision."

On Madison's last visit to Philadelphia, the esteemed colonist and philanthropist had impressed him. Franklin's sharp wit never failed to hit the mark.

"What does he say?"

" 'Lord Loudon's campaigns were frivolous, expensive, and disgraceful to our nation beyond conception. He was always

105

busy but accomplishing nothing. He was like St. George on a tavern sign, always on horseback and never riding on.'"

"Are we referring to the inept Lord Loudon again?" Captain Rogers, joining them, sat down then propped his boot on the edge of the bench. He rested his arm across one knee and winked. "I cannot think of another man who would be worthy of such a compliment."

Madison chuckled. "Lewis just brought news about Loudon being recalled to England. We were about to celebrate. Would you like to join us?"

"You think I would miss the chance to rejoice in being rid of that tyrant?" Rogers guffawed. "He has been a thorn in my side since I first took command of my own troops."

"Not exactly on the best of terms, you two?" Madison teased.

Rogers coughed. "Let's just say that England can have him and mete out whatever punishment they can concoct for his lack of action here in the colonies."

"And here I thought you had learned a great deal from the commander," Lewis chimed in.

"Oh, I did," Rogers countered. "I learned what *not* to do in planning an attack and how *not* to follow through with plans. I also learned how to avoid battle and assign senseless work to troops to keep them busy while our enemy disposes of worthy soldiers and comrades."

"Had it not been for his disregard of Colonel Washington's advice after Braddock was killed two years ago, we might have secured more forts along the western frontier." Madison tapped his journal with his index finger. "Instead, we lost several of them to the French and have been fighting ever since to regain our stronghold."

Lewis turned toward the other two and groaned in frustration. "Bumblingly true to form, Loudon dithered while the French concentrated a fleet at Louisburg, far superior to the British numbers he attempted to gather."

"And while the French were doing that, Loudon had his men plant cabbage of all things!" Rogers whacked the back of the bench and the vibration rumbled against Madison's back. "What did he think he was doing? Preparing a garden?"

"At least he returned to New York before taking an ill-prepared army north," Madison pointed out. "The results would have been disastrous."

Rogers gritted his teeth. "Yes, but following that coward's retreat, the French took Fort William Henry. We lost a lot of good men there."

Momentary silence followed. Madison willed away the plaguing thoughts of that horrible loss last summer.

Matthew resumed the conversation. "When Loudon insisted that our colonial governments quarter his troops, even though they had yet to lend any aid to our cause, I thought there would be rebellion."

"But his threats and bullying gave him his way," Madison added.

"He was the most inept, the most incompetent, the most arrogant, and the most sluggish commander I have ever met."

Madison reached up and squeezed Rogers's shoulder. "And he is no longer a problem for any of us."

Rogers composed himself and gestured toward the article Matthew held. "Does that paper say anything about who England is sending as his replacement?"

Matthew glanced down. "Secretary of state William Pitt," he supplied.

"Now *that* is a man with strong leadership."

Madison regarded Rogers with curiosity. He had only just learned of Pitt's plans to launch an attack on Louisburg in the recent officers' meeting. "You have heard of him?"

"Not in regard to the war, but in the political world, he is rumored to be quite adept at taking charge." Rogers grinned. "Sounds like my kind of man."

Matthew and Madison both laughed. Rogers might be a little rough around the edges, but his devotion could not be matched.

"Time will tell," Madison replied.

"He cannot be any worse than Loudon."

"We can hope," Lewis said, echoing what they all wished.

Rogers removed his foot from the bench and straightened. "Well, I had best be getting back to my men. With Pitt on his way, they will no doubt be in need of some good scouts. And my rangers are perfect for the job."

Madison and Lewis both stood and saluted their compatriot.

"Perhaps we will finally see some victories on our side of the fighting."

"If I have any say in the matter, we will," Rogers answered and was gone.

Lewis reached out and tipped up the journal in Madison's hands. "So, did I interrupt another letter to your lady friend in New Castle?"

"An attempt at one, anyway."

"How long has it been?"

Madison looked down at the journal and recalled the long, lonely winter months. "Almost six months."

Matthew looked incredulous. "And you have received nothing from her either in all this time?"

"Courier travel is light at best during the winter," he reminded his friend. "And planting, harvesting, and farm work keep Elanna rather occupied."

"It did not help much that you also had to endure frostbite on your fingers a few weeks ago, either." Matthew looked Madison square in the eyes. "But I owe my life to you for coming out to find me."

"You would have done the same for me."

He winked. "Of course I would. Life would be rather dull if I could not tease you about pining for a lady hundreds of miles away."

"It is good to see you back to your old self again." Madison grinned and clapped Matthew on the back.

"Good to be back." He stepped away. "Now, I do believe I smell a piece of corn bread and hear a roast chicken calling my name."

Madison shook his head as he watched Matthew head in the direction of the fort. His own stomach rumbled in response, but he ignored it in light of wanting to finish the letter to Elanna. Unable to focus in that spot, he started walking south along the riverbank until he cleared the edge of the fort.

The Hudson flowed slow and easy at this juncture below the bend on its way to providing a water source to the ever-expanding town of Fort Edward a few hundred feet farther to the south. A few ascending hills gave the fort its key position overlooking the town that had grown exponentially since the start of the war, now only superceded by Boston and New York City. That growth reminded him of the increased industry in Wilmington, just north of New Castle. Madison wished for an end to this war so he could get on with his life and do something he actually enjoyed.

Finding a secluded spot, he sat in the grass and crossed his legs to provide a surface upon which to write. He pulled out his pen and once again resumed his letter:

How desperate I am to share with you everything about my experiences up here. But we must remain mindful of prying eyes that might happen upon our written exchange.

So many words fill my heart and mind, yet I find myself warring within about which ones to write to you. It has been far too long since we have been in communication with each other, and I pray you are still in good health. The winter here took several more good men. Others we lost due to injuries from battle. Thanks be to the good Lord for seeing fit to spare my lieutenant from death's clutches after losing his way during a sudden snowstorm. I have Him to thank as well for saving my hands from frostbite as a result of the search to find the lieutenant. Had I been able to write, I would have.

He prayed Elanna would forgive him for the lapse in time between letters. Without knowing what prevented him from keeping in touch, any manner of thought could have entered her mind. Hopefully, she wasn't worrying or fearing that some tragedy had befallen him. That concern drove him to finish this letter now and get it to Benjamin at the next courier delivery.

Life on the battlefield and at the front lines of this war is not a life for any man, but I know my skills are a benefit to the cause. Until we can be assured that the savage way of life of the French is under control, our presence in this frontier is in great demand. It feels like an eternity since I last saw your face, but the details of it remain firmly fixed in my mind. Your soft voice, your sweet nature, and the memory of your incurable taste for adventure have kept me going day in and day out, despite the less-than-glorious circumstances surrounding our efforts. Maintaining my focus on the task at hand has been difficult at times, when all I want to do is return to New Castle and enjoy your company once more.

Even now, Madison could recall every feature of Elanna's

face. From her eyes' deep shade of gray to her lips the color of ripe berries he'd found the other day, and the image of her feminine curves, each detail was burned into his memory. The fact that she would soon be seventeen only made him yearn for her that much more. He prayed with everything in him that she had not found another suitor more to her liking and that the promises she made a year ago would still hold true.

> *Time and distance have a way of changing things, but you can be assured that my feelings for you have not. They are stronger now than they have ever been. With each battle I fight and each day that passes, I know it is one more that brings me closer to the time when I will see you again. Even now, we are making plans for a different type of attack than we have yet attempted. With Lord Loudon recalled to England and his replacement ready to succeed where Loudon failed, we are poised with great potential for a significant win should everything go according to plan. On the heels of the atrocities committed by the Indians last summer, I would like nothing better than to return their barbaric attacks with some of the same from our regiments.*
>
> *Our militia and soldiers are preparing even now for this plan devised by our new commander. With Colonel Washington keeping the French and Indians at bay in Pennsylvania, we will move to secure the lands in other areas.*

Madison was careful to avoid mention of any specific direction or location. The worst thing that could happen would be for this letter to be intercepted and Pitt's attack plan discovered before the time came to enact it. Marching northeast toward Louisburg and joining more than ten thousand men, plus amassing a Royal Navy fleet of 150 transport vessels out of Halifax to approach from the waterways, they were sure to catch the French by surprise. They needed to take the fortress at Louisburg in order to gain access to the St. Lawrence River and further pave the way toward Quebec. Their enemy might have enjoyed their superior position while Loudon commanded the British forces, but William Pitt and Major General Jeffrey Amherst wouldn't be so accommodating.

As I sit along the banks of this river, I very much long to walk with you again along the Delaware and see the vibrant colors of spring in full bloom. Far too many seasons have passed during our separation. When we are together again, I vow to make up for all of that and more. I pray you will remain receptive to my attention.

Now, my brief respite has come to an end, and thus so must my letter. May God be with you and continue to keep you safe while I am unable to do so. And if you do not receive another letter from me before the time, allow me to send my best wishes on the celebration of your next birthday. You have become a woman while I have been away, and I regret not being there to see that transformation take place. You no doubt have caught the attention of many young men of your acquaintance. I can only pray that you afford me the opportunity to stand before you again before you decide on another.

In the meantime, I shall count the days until we are together again. Know that my heart continues to be yours.

Fondly,
Madison

He folded the pages and slipped them into the envelope, then sealed it tight. Unless his sight had betrayed him,

Benjamin had arrived just in time. The courier could take his letter with him on his next journey south. If only Madison knew how Elanna felt.

ૐ

"Thank you, Miss Hanssen, for a delightful afternoon." Mr. Witherspoon stood next to the carriage and offered his hand to help Elanna down. It was her first unchaperoned visit with the journalist, and thus far, their time together had been pleasant.

She placed her gloved fingers in his and stepped softly to the ground. The sun shone bright and warm, and the clear blue sky spread for miles without a cloud in sight. Despite the enjoyment she felt in the journalist's presence, she couldn't ignore the feeling that it would have been that much better with Madison at her side.

"If I may," Mr. Witherspoon's voice interrupted her musings, "I would like to invite you to accompany me to an outdoor musical performance two weeks hence."

Elanna tilted her head and regarded him with a sideways glance. He had been every bit the gentleman during their time together. After taking her along the Christina River, he had veered south and driven toward New Castle with the Delaware River to their left. The horses had been given their heads and allowed to lumber at their own pace as Mr. Witherspoon shared story after story from his adventures. She had enjoyed the afternoon more than she thought she would. But was it enough for her to continue spending time with him?

After careful consideration, she nodded. "I shall look forward to the evening, Mr. Witherspoon. Thank you for thinking of me."

He raised her hand to his lips. "Thinking of you comes second only to my work, Miss Hanssen."

Elanna warmed under his flattery, but something about

the smooth way in which he delivered the compliment didn't sit well with her. Until she could put her finger on what that was, she endeavored to keep her distance.

He looked over his shoulder at the Greyson residence. "Are you certain they are expecting you?"

She stepped forward and unlatched the gate to the front walk. "Yes. Chelcy and I have a prearranged time when we meet."

"Good day, then, Miss Hanssen." He bowed slightly and stepped into the carriage.

"Good day, Mr. Witherspoon," she replied as he snapped the reins and drove off.

She turned toward the front door in time to see Chelcy open it and step outside. Her friend's eyes caught sight of the departing carriage and a questioning look replaced the one of delight upon seeing Elanna.

"Are you entertaining other suitors besides my cousin?"

Elanna quelled the defensiveness that rose to the surface at Chelcy's accusatory tone. "That is Mr. Witherspoon, and he was kind enough to bring me here after our meeting earlier this afternoon."

"The journalist?" Chelcy placed an arm around Elanna and guided her inside. "Why did you not say so in the first place?"

A servant stood by and offered two cups of lemonade. Elanna welcomed the refreshment as she followed Chelcy to the gardens out back.

"I have only recently been spending a more substantial time with Mr. Witherspoon, so I did not feel it bore any importance to mention it to you."

Chelcy stopped and Elanna almost bumped into her. "Do you mean to tell me that you are spending time with him for more than information pertaining to the war?"

Elanna looked away and stepped around Chelcy toward

the path leading to the table and benches. "He has such fascinating stories to share, and I enjoy his company."

"But you are not considering anything else, are you?"

"I cannot say for certain," Elanna replied honestly. She hadn't yet been able to make sense of her feelings toward Mr. Witherspoon. After Madison's last letter and strong declaration of his own feelings, she couldn't be more perplexed.

Chelcy quickened her steps to catch up to her and grabbed hold of her arm. "You are going to have to do better than that, my dear friend. A response such as that might well appease your family or someone who does not know you as well as I, but I will not move from this spot until you tell me everything."

How had she gotten so lucky to have Chelcy for a friend? A slight grin found its way to her lips as she took in the comical determination on Chelcy's face. Had she not been holding a cup in one hand, she no doubt would have planted both fists firmly on her hips in anticipation of Elanna's answer.

Knowing she didn't have a choice, Elanna shared all of the ups and downs and uncertainties that had plagued her for the past year. Some of it, Chelcy already knew from other times they had spent together, but Elanna filled in all of the blanks now.

"Madison's latest letter has left me more confused than ever."

Chelcy took a seat on one bench, and Elanna sat opposite her.

"How so?" her friend asked.

She paused and tried to decide how much to share. Some of what he said she knew he wouldn't want shared with anyone else, but surely it wouldn't hurt to talk about it in generic terms.

"He was rather adamant about his desire to be with me

again and lamented the time we have been apart."

Chelcy smiled. "That sounds like my cousin."

"But before I received that letter, I had spoken with Mr. Witherspoon just after the spring thaw and learned that Madison's name had appeared on reports from the battles up north."

"Is that not a good thing?"

"The mention was not flattering," Elanna said with a sigh. "They painted Madison in a rather unfavorable light, saying that he had committed heinous acts against the French and Indians and had even been responsible for the death of several of his men due to his complete disregard of safety measures during attacks."

Chelcy arched her back and braced her hands on the table. "Now that does not sound like Madison in any way!"

Her protest startled Elanna and almost upset the drinks on the table.

"That is what I have tried to tell myself many times, but something Madison wrote in this last letter gave me pause."

"What was it?"

"He said that he would like to return the atrocities of the French and Indians with some of the same from his own regiment."

"Considering everything that has taken place," Chelcy began with a calm tone, "and the stories you have heard or read, can you honestly find fault with such ardor?"

Elanna brushed a nonexistent bit of dust from her sleeve and took a deep breath. "No," she said with shame. "But neither can I ignore the facts that Mr. Witherspoon has presented. He receives news from several reliable sources."

"Have you actually seen these reports and read them for yourself?"

Now why hadn't she thought of that?

"No," Elanna answered.

She had been so distraught over the thought that Madison could be less than he had presented himself to be that she hadn't taken the time to explore the issue from all sides.

"Then I suggest that before you form assumptions about the truth of Madison's words, you ask Mr. Witherspoon to provide proof of his accusations. Otherwise, I might be inclined to assume that he has ulterior motives."

"He has been nothing but a gentleman at every meeting we have had."

"Even a wolf can conceal his true nature beneath sheep's clothing for a time. Before long, though, the truth will be known."

Elanna reached across for Chelcy's hands and clasped them in hers. "What would I do without you?"

"Suffer in anguish and find it impossible to make up your own mind about the men in your life," she parried with a grin.

A giggle bubbled in Elanna's chest. She hadn't felt this lighthearted in weeks. For the remainder of their visit, they spoke of the changes in town and the continued fear of a French attack from the water, but the reassurance from the assembly that their ports were safe helped stave that concern. Nevertheless, the colonists still remained alert, and despite the effects of the war, made certain to keep to their daily activities.

As Elanna rode home in the back of the wagon after Papa and Edric met her, following their meeting in town, she had plenty of time to consider Chelcy's words regarding Mr. Witherspoon. Still unable to decide one way or the other, she prayed the truth would be revealed before it was too late.

ten

"We have met with great success in our capture of the fortress at Louisburg," Major General Amherst announced at the officers' meeting in mid-August.

Although casualties were minimal for the British and the colonists who went north to fight, Madison still counted with a heavy heart the number of injured as the transport returned them to Fort Edward and the hospital there. So much killing. So much anger and hatred.

"Our defeats at Fort Carillon and Fort Duquesne were unfortunate," Amherst continued. "But we are preparing a three-part attack both in the regions to our north along the Canadian border and the western edge of the Ohio Valley."

"If it had not been for Abercrombie's incompetence, our numbers alone would have won us Carillon," Rogers whispered to Madison.

"You only say that because your rangers paved the way for the British, and the result was not the one you wanted," Madison whispered back.

"It was the marching columns that caused the problem. If Abercrombie had heeded my suggestions, they would have avoided the narrow road that caused them to be scattered about too far and wide to control. They could have regrouped and taken a stand, rather than chasing the French after driving them off. We lost a good man out there. Lord Howe and his light infantry could have served us well."

"Perhaps you will have another opportunity with our next attack."

"I will guarantee it," Rogers vowed.

Amherst's voice rose, and Madison caught the warning look aimed in his direction. He tapped one finger several times on the table in front of Rogers as a signal to be quiet. They could not afford to be dismissed from the meeting and possibly overlooked when it came time for command selections to take place.

"In a few weeks, at the request of Brigadier Forbes, Major James Grant of Ballindalloch, acting commander of the 77th Regiment of Foot and Montgomerie's Highlanders, will lead 750 men to Fort Duquesne on a nocturnal reconnaissance mission ahead of General John Forbes's main column of six thousand men. Colonel Washington will lead a contingent of two thousand Virginian and Pennsylvanian militia. They will move from there to defend Fort Ligonier against any further French attacks."

On the one hand, Madison wished he could be sent to the western corridor where he might have the good fortune of fighting side by side with Colonel Washington. On the other, he was needed here in the Hudson Valley as they sought to gain control of the northern reaches of the territory.

"Lieutenant Colonel John Bradstreet will lead an army of over three thousand men north toward Fort Frontenac at the eastern end of Lake Ontario where it meets the St. Lawrence River. We will assign smaller contingents to be part of his numbers." Amherst walked among the officers and looked each one of them in the eye, his commanding presence and determined look making every man present sit up and take notice. "The success of this attack is imperative. With it, we will cut off one of the two major communication and supply lines between the key eastern centers of Montreal and Quebec City and the western territories of France. From there, we will make our way to Quebec." He clapped his hands together, and the startling smack of skin meeting skin reverberated through the ranks. "Gentleman, our success or failure is up to you."

After a discussion of more details and planned maneuvers, the meeting adjourned. Madison and Rogers stepped outside into the baking heat of the overhead sun. They headed for the water station and drank heavily of the refreshing liquid.

Rogers wiped his mouth on his sleeve. "I hope they mount a better attack plan this time than on Carillon."

Madison retrieved his handkerchief and mopped up the excess water. "From the sound of things inside," he nodded toward the closed door, "I am guessing they have learned from Abercrombie's mistakes."

"They should open their eyes and realize how much stronger their forces would be if they put me in charge and let me make full use of my rangers."

"You know very well that you will never attain a higher rank if you continue to plague your commanding officers and fly in the face of their orders."

Rogers capitulated. "Yes, I know, but that does not mean I cannot hope."

Madison laughed. "No, in that regard, you are correct. Hope is about the only thing we have left these days, although our recent victory at Louisburg has done a lot to bolster the spirits of our troops."

"That is because they employed true military tactics and made good use of their brains instead of falling back on the ineffective marching lines."

"Thanks to you and your rangers, of course." Madison bowed slightly and gave a wide sweep of his arm in front of Rogers.

"Do not forget the assistance of the colonial militia as well," Rogers added. "Their desire to maintain their freedom goes a long way toward guaranteeing their devotion."

"How could I?" Madison retorted. "I am proud to call myself one of them."

⋅∞⋅

The weeks and months passed as the three-part attack unfolded. Although Fort Duquesne remained in the hands of the French, forcing Grant and Washington to redirect their troops to Fort Ligonier, the attack on Fort Frontenac met with great success. Madison almost didn't believe his eyes when they stormed the fort and found such a measly number of French in position to defend it.

As spoils from their attack, the British seized eight hundred thousand pounds of goods from the trading post, including sixty pieces of cannon, sixteen small mortars, and an immense quantity of merchandise and provisions that would sustain their troops for a good, long while. With winter fast approaching, those supplies would come in handy. Madison could already feel the chill in the air as the first couple weeks of December signaled the beginning of another lonely cold season.

He had hoped to have a letter from Elanna to warm him on the inside, but after the last one he received, the chances of that were slim. Dated 27 October 1758, her brief letter was the shortest since they had begun correspondence. It surprised him to read the questions she had regarding his role in the war. Elanna appeared to doubt the truths he had shared with her about his exploits and command experiences. Even her response to his heartfelt words had seemed cool and lacking emotion:

> *I appreciate you sharing your heart with me, and I*
> *hope to have the opportunity to do the same. It is not easy*
> *maintaining our relationship with the miles that separate us.*
> *Communication can be interrupted or misinterpreted at any*
> *time, and we are forced to take what we have at face value. I*
> *wish I could say more, but we are in the middle of the harvest,*

*and my assistance is needed as we prepare for another winter.
Thankfully, I have Mr. Witherspoon's accounts to help me fill
in the holes left by our careful correspondence.*

She brought her letter to a close with just a few more words
about praying for him and wishing him success in his battles.
Although filled with the standard concern and cordiality, it
lacked the depth of emotion he had come to expect from
Elanna's letters. Something wasn't right, but he didn't know
what. He didn't know how to fix it, either.

"They burned it!" The frantic voice of a colonel sounded
from the main courtyard of the fort. "The French burned
Fort Duquesne."

Madison rushed from his quarters and down the side steps
to join the others in hearing the rest of the news. Elanna's
letter was momentarily forgotten.

"This message just arrived. They burned their own fort
and left under a cover of darkness. When word reached
our troops, they headed for the fort and marched up to the
smoldering remains, appalled at the sight that greeted them.
The French-allied Indians had cut off the heads of many of
the dead Highlanders left to rot by the French and impaled
them on the sharp stakes on top of the fort walls, with their
kilts displayed below."

Madison's stomach turned at the mental pictures created by
the announcement. He sent up a prayer for the families of those
men when word was delivered of their fate. Yet another example
of the Indian brutality and gruesome warfare practices. It was no
wonder the French had absorbed so many of those tactics into
their own attack plans. With as many successes as they had seen,
they would continue with what worked.

"Despite the atrocities, we now have command of the fort.
It looks like the tide is turning in our favor after all," Lewis

spoke from behind Madison's left shoulder.

"Yes," Madison agreed. "The securing of Fort Duquesne affords us complete control of the western fringes of the Ohio Valley. Add to that our victory at Frontenac, and we are slowly gaining ground against the French strongholds in this area."

"Before long, we will be the ones advancing and sending the French on a retreat back to where they came from."

"In light of this recent report, I long for that day to arrive." Madison still tried to rid his mind of the horrific images, as dwelling on them only increased his anger.

"I overheard Amherst talking with several other generals just now, and it seems the French and Canadian garrisons have been moved closer to Quebec, Montreal, and the French western forts."

Madison draped an arm across Matthew's shoulders. "Then, that is where we will no doubt be concentrating our efforts this winter."

Lewis stood at attention, causing Madison's arm to fall back to his side, and saluted. "You give the orders, sir, and I will follow without question."

"I have not even received my orders for these presumed attacks."

Matthew grinned and gave Madison a knowing wink. "But when you do, be sure to come find me."

"I would not enter battle without you."

Once the excitement about Fort Duquesne died down, Madison returned to his quarters to start preparing for the attacks that were sure to come. If only he could solve the dilemma of Elanna as easily as he could devise a battle plan. Then her words might not haunt him as much.

&

"Elanna!" Edric called from the front of the house. "You have a visitor."

Who would be coming to see her in the middle of winter? Surely not Mr. Witherspoon or Chelcy. Wrapping her cloak around her and enfolding her mitten-covered hands in the warmth of her muff, she pushed open the door and stepped outside. A frigid blast of air hit her face. She closed her eyes against the onslaught and waited for it to pass so she could identify the person who had come to call.

"Benjamin!" Her heart leaped in her chest. He had never journeyed this far south during the winter before.

"Miss Hanssen," the courier replied. "I made haste in order to deliver this to you." He held out a letter with Madison's distinct scrawl on the outside envelope.

Elanna took it, but her voice caught in her throat as she attempted to thank him. She could only stare at the missive, several different scenarios running through her mind about what she might find inside. With the way she had left things in her last letter, she wouldn't blame him if he decided to put an end to their correspondence.

"He is fine and healthy, if that is causing you concern," Benjamin assured her.

She managed a half smile as she scrutinized the envelope from all angles. "Thank you. I confess that I do worry about Major Scott's welfare, especially when word from him is so scarce."

"Word from anyone is scarce during the winter months," Edric chimed in.

"Which is exactly why I wanted to get this to you on my way back north," Benjamin supplied. "My route lagged a little this time around because of the fierce battles taking place in the Hudson Valley."

Elanna startled at hearing this. That was where Madison was! "You are certain Major Scott remains all right?"

"When I last spoke with him, he had just returned from

an attack at Louisburg near Nova Scotia." He nodded toward the letter she held. "You will no doubt read all about it in his words. I am sure they are far better than mine."

This brought a full smile to Elanna's lips. "I do appreciate your taking the time to deliver this, Benjamin. Please come in and warm yourself by the fire. I will have a cup of hot cider brought to you as well."

Receiving no argument from the courier, she led the way with Benjamin following and Edric bringing up the rear. After seeing to Benjamin's comforts, Elanna slipped away to her room to read Madison's letter:

14 December 1758
My dearest Elanna,
   I will not attempt to conceal my hurt upon receiving your last missive and finding it devoid of the deep emotion you had conveyed so adequately in previous correspondence. Your words and the impersonal manner in which you imparted them plagued me for days as I endeavored to interpret the meaning behind them. At the very least, I sought to determine the cause that led you to respond in such a way to my heartfelt words when last I wrote.

She knew the moment she let go of the letter, right as the harvest was ending, that she should have given her words more consideration before sealing the envelope. Despite what Mr. Witherspoon had told her, Madison deserved more than her impulsive reaction to the doubt and uncertainties floating around in her mind. She wasn't even 100 percent certain that what the journalist told her was true. Yet rather than give Madison the benefit of the doubt as Chelcy advised her to do, she had hastily jotted down a few disjointed thoughts and sent the note on its way. No wonder Madison was confused.

I have recently returned from a successful siege of a fortress to the far north, one that has guaranteed British control of the waterways in that area and blocked passage of French ships farther inland. With so many defeats over the past two years, our morale has been quite low. It had begun to affect the level at which we fought and often caused us to make mistakes which cost us the lives of many men.

Now, however, the troops have rallied and found their fervor again for seeing an end to this war. It has made a distinct difference in the overall attitudes of those garrisoned at the fort and those across the river at the hospital or living in the barracks. Word has even spread to the town down the hill, and the colonists there have celebrated right alongside us. On more than one occasion, we have been invited into the homes of many and given a warm meal or fresh bread. Those are things not found in abundance during our times of fighting. Far too often we go without and find ourselves in a weakened state. So the added sustenance provided by the generous townspeople is a welcome gift.

She paused and read over his words again. The way in which he shared about his life at the fort and experiences in battle painted a clear picture for Elanna of all that he endured on a daily basis. She felt drawn in by the words he chose and a unique connection formed between them that spanned the miles. If only she could be certain. He seemed sincere enough in what he wrote, but that nagging doubt in the back of her mind wouldn't go away.

As we head into the winter months once more, I cannot help but turn my thoughts toward you and your family and the celebrations that are taking place in your home. From your letter last year, I can still smell the cider and unique

spices that permeate the air. I can see the roaring fires that
warm your rooms and imagine the festivities as you gather
with your family and friends to celebrate Christmas. It only
makes me long for the chance to be with you again, but I try
to keep those thoughts at bay, lest I lose my concentration and
commit a mistake that could cost me in lives.

I still do not know what has led to the change in tone in
your letter to me, but I pray that you resolve whatever has
caused this shift and return to the fanciful young woman
who has endeared herself to me in so many ways. Until we
once again have the opportunity to write and receive each
other's letters, I remain most devotedly and faithfully yours.

Madison

A lone tear slid down Elanna's cheek at Madison's closing
words. Every doubt she felt was in direct opposition to the
man portrayed in the letter she held. Mr. Witherspoon had
shared details with her that went against the character of
the man she had believed Madison to be. But the journalist
was here, and Madison wasn't. Who was she to believe?
She wished she had some form of concrete proof one way
or the other. Then she might be able to lay to rest her inner
struggle.

❧

Several weeks later, Elanna received another letter. Only this
time it wasn't from Madison. It was from Mr. Witherspoon.
Inside, she found only one sheet of paper with the words,
I am truly sorry written at the top. Below those words in
Witherspoon's recognizable script, she read:

Major Madison Scott disobeyed orders during the recent
skirmish against the French at Fort Frontenac. Despite
several warnings, he disregarded the command of his

superiors as he led his regiment on a brutal and savage siege
of the already conquered French. This attack following their
surrender earned Scott the scorn of his fellow soldiers.

Elanna covered her gasp with a hand over her mouth. The
last time the journalist had tried to tell her about Madison, he
hadn't provided any proof. But now he had. There it was, in
black and white, yet still in the journalist's own handwriting. A
part of her felt she could no longer deny it, although her heart
continued to protest. The Madison she thought she knew was
not the same man in this report. Who was telling the truth?

The time had come for her to put the questions to him
directly, but Elanna didn't know if she could.

eleven

"Mama, can I speak with you about something important?" Elanna asked as she stepped down into the kitchen. Its warmth provided immediate relief from the chill throughout the rest of the house. She prayed spring would come soon.

Mama looked up from the cast-iron pot hung on the crane where she stirred the stew for dinner. She reached for a pinch of salt from the salt box and sprinkled it into the pot. "Of course." She peered at Elanna and a frown formed on her lips. "Tell me what has you so vexed."

Elanna dropped into the nearest chair and slumped over the table in the center of the kitchen.

"Sit up straight, dear," Mama reprimanded as she placed the utensil she used into the spoon rack that hung on the wall next to the fireplace.

Elanna complied, then unfolded the note Mr. Witherspoon had sent to her three days ago. It had taken her this long to figure out what she needed to do. Distracted by the dilemma, somehow she had still managed to complete her chores without making any mistakes. But it hadn't been easy.

"Mama, you know I have been writing to Major Scott while he has been away fighting in the war."

"Yes." Mama stepped away from the hearth, wiped her hands on her apron, and reached for a knife from the knife box to start cutting vegetables for the stew. "Although your father and I wish we had met him during his visit here, we are still in support of your correspondence." She covered one of Elanna's hands with her own. "In fact, we are quite pleased."

Elanna tried hard to fight back the tears that threatened to cloud her vision. If only Mama knew what she was about to say. After everything she had shared with them about Madison, this news would come as a shock.

She sniffed. "You are also aware of my meetings with Mr. Witherspoon in Wilmington from time to time."

Mama pursed her lips, her disapproval clear. "Even though the one instance you spent time with him alone went against my better judgment, yes."

Elanna took a deep breath and plunged ahead. "Mama, I have received some rather distressing news about Major Scott from Mr. Witherspoon. It first came in the spring of last year, and then again three days ago." She smoothed her hands across the paper in front of her. "At first, I refused to believe it could be true, but with this most recent revelation, I do not know what to believe."

This caught Mama's attention. She stopped the rhythmic motion of the knife and focused on Elanna. "What distressing news have you received?"

She handed the letter to Mama, who took it and read the contents. At first, Mama chewed on her lower lip. Then she knitted her brows. Several other emotions crossed her face before she finally spoke.

"Has this Mr. Witherspoon ever given you a reason to doubt the veracity of his findings?"

A quick memory of the way the journalist had avoided a question she once asked flashed in her mind, but Elanna ignored it. "None as of yet."

"And do you feel you can trust him more than Major Scott?"

Elanna let out an exasperated breath. "That is the problem, Mama. I am not certain which man I should believe more. From every conversation and all appearances, Major Scott has proven to be a man full of integrity, honesty, and true devotion. It was those traits that appealed to me right from the start."

Mama handed the note back to Elanna and resumed chopping. "And now you find that you doubt the manner in which he has presented himself to you?"

"I find that without him here to prove or disprove the reports I am hearing, it is difficult to know the real truth."

"Have you asked him about the reports or shared your feelings with him?"

"No," Elanna said, her voice filled with chagrin. "That is where I am uncertain. Because I do not know if he is telling the truth, how am I to know if the reply he gives me is not more of the same?"

Elanna stood and walked to the hearth. After using the towel to move the crane from over the fire, she took the spoon from the rack and stirred the contents. Mama turned and dumped an apron-full of vegetables into the mix.

"And what does Mr. Witherspoon have to say about all of this?"

Elanna stared into the liquid depths of the murky brown stew and watched the vegetables get swallowed as she stirred. That was just how she felt with her thoughts all jumbled and she unable to separate them.

"Mr. Witherspoon has assured me on more than one occasion that he means me no ill will and that he regrets he has to be the one to share this information with me."

Mama bent forward and used her apron to pull down the door to the brick oven, built into the side of the fireplace. With a flat board, she retrieved the fresh-baked bread and set it on the counter to cool. As Elanna continued to stir, Mama sliced the loaf of bread.

"How well would you say that you know this journalist?"

Now, how should she answer this question? "He has always conducted himself properly in my presence."

"And is there anyone else among your acquaintance who can vouch for *his* integrity or honor?"

Elanna turned from the pot. "Why do you doubt him, Mama? You have never met him."

Mama shrugged. "I am merely speculating on the purity of his motives, my dear."

"That is the very same thing Chelcy said to me the other day," Elanna murmured.

Mama placed the bread in a basket on the table and covered it with a towel. "To which you replied?"

"I promised Chelcy that I would give it careful consideration and weigh everything from all sides."

"It seems to be that your friend is quite astute." Mama placed her hands on Elanna's shoulders and turned her so they were face-to-face. "I believe the best thing for you to do is write to Major Scott and share your feelings and doubts with him. Tell him about the reports and what Mr. Witherspoon has provided to you. Let Major Scott be the one to decide how to respond." She cupped Elanna's chin in her hand and offered a soft smile. "After nearly three years of correspondence, you at least owe him that."

Elanna threw her arms around Mama and hugged her tight as a couple of tears slid down her cheeks. Mama returned the embrace and stroked Elanna's hair. When Elanna pulled away, she wiped her tears and smiled.

"Thank you, Mama. I will go and write Major Scott right away."

Mama touched Elanna's cheek. "You are more than welcome, my daughter. I will pray that you find relief from this inner battle soon."

Elanna headed for the doorway into the hall, but Mama's

voice stopped her on the step.

"Whatever happens, your papa and I know you will make the right decision."

She tilted her head in response as love for Mama softened her features. Tears glistened in Mama's eyes, but she blinked them away.

"Now, off you go," she said with a swish of her apron. "You have a letter to write."

"Yes, Mama," Elanna replied and headed up to her room.

Once there, she sat at her desk and raised the lid for access to her ink and paper. Pressing the tip of the feather against her lips, she labored over how she should begin. Her heart told her one thing, and her head told her another. Considering the content, she let her heart win.

11 March 1759
My dearest Madison,

Before I begin, I need to ask for your forgiveness for the abrupt manner in which I composed my previous letter. After receiving your reply, I realized how confused you must have been when you read my words. So please allow me the opportunity to explain. I pray you will be receptive to what I am about to share.

In more than one of my letters, I have written to you about the journalist whose acquaintance I have made here in Wilmington. We have met several times, and he has been quite thorough in providing me with additional information regarding the war. Because of the need for you and I to be careful about how much we reveal in our letters, Mr. Witherspoon has been able to answer many of my questions when I knew you would be unable to give those details. I must admit, our meetings have gone a long way toward appeasing my insatiable curiosity regarding your experiences up north.

But it is the reports Mr. Witherspoon has shared with me during recent meetings that have caused me distress. And that is why I am writing to you now.

From there, the letter flowed with all of Elanna's feelings and doubts pouring onto the paper. Page after page was filled with her questions and beseeching Madison to put her mind at rest. When she finished, she read it over again to be sure everything sounded all right; then she slipped it into an envelope and applied the seal.

As Elanna held the letter in her hand, she felt a momentary pang of fear that Madison's response might not be what she wanted it to be. But that was all in God's hands now. She could no more control the outcome of her relationship with Madison than she could the war he was fighting up north. She had done her part. Now, she had to let go and let God work, no matter how difficult that might be.

❧

Elanna walked down the gleaming hardwood hallway toward Mr. Witherspoon's office and stood in the doorway before knocking to announce her presence. He sat at his desk, hard at work, writing something that appeared important from the way he concentrated on each word he put on the paper.

"There! Done," he exclaimed and blotted the ink.

"Is that your latest article for the *Journal*?" Elanna asked as she stepped into the room.

Mr. Witherspoon started and shuffled several papers on his desk before slipping the one he had just completed between two other sheets. He offered her a wide smile and stood to welcome her.

"Miss Hanssen, how good it is to see you again."

Elanna approached to stand before him.

"I have just come from New Castle after posting a letter

with the courier, and Edric offered to drive me here for a quick visit."

The journalist clasped her hands in his and beamed. "And I am glad you have come."

At this close proximity, Elanna could see a fine sheen of perspiration on his forehead. What had he been doing when she arrived? She didn't know if it would be improper to ask or if she should allow him to share when he was ready. So she remained silent.

"Tell me, is your brother waiting outside?"

"He is speaking with one of the typesetters. I promised him the visit would not be long."

Mr. Witherspoon regarded her with a question in his eyes. "Did you have a particular purpose in mind in coming to call?"

"I wanted to thank you for the report you sent me earlier this month, regarding Major Scott during one of the attacks on the French forts the previous autumn."

Immediate regret filled his eyes, and Elanna couldn't decide if he was sincere or merely adept at controlling his emotions and playing whatever role was necessary.

"I did not enjoy the fact that I had to share that with you. Your affection for Major Scott has not been lost on me, and I feared how you would respond upon learning the truth about his actions up north."

Elanna moved to sit in one of the chairs, and Mr. Witherspoon took the other.

"It did come as a shock, I confess. When you originally shared news with me last year but neglected to provide an actual report, I had my doubts." She watched the journalist for any reaction that might reveal something other than concern for her welfare. "With the real article written by you in my hands, it made things a bit clearer."

"For that, you are quite welcome. It pains me to see you

struggle in such a way when I could provide you with answers to your questions and help ease your tortured mind."

"And I appreciate your assistance in that regard."

"So," Mr. Witherspoon began as he scooted to the edge of the chair and placed one hand on the arm of hers. "Have you made up your mind, then? Have you decided to bid farewell to Major Scott in light of what I have told you?"

He seemed a bit too eager for Elanna's peace of mind. She needed to tread carefully and choose her words with caution. "In truth, I have decided to write to Major Scott and present the reports to him exactly as you have shared them with me."

A flash of fear appeared in his eyes before he concealed it and regained his air of nonchalance.

"That is the letter I mentioned a few moments ago. After much debate in my mind, and after a beneficial conversation with my mother, I realized that I could not in good conscience disregard Major Scott without allowing him the opportunity to defend himself."

He leaned forward as an earnestness overtook his calm assurance. "But how can you be certain he will not continue to falsify the reports or misrepresent the truth in his response to you?"

Elanna looked out the window behind his desk and watched the distorted images pass in front of it. "I do not know for sure, but I at least owe him the chance to explain, regardless of his answer."

"And what if his reply confirms everything I have said? Will you surrender this foolish notion and accept my affections instead?"

She gasped. Did he just say what she thought she heard him say? With a hand on her heart, she exclaimed, "Mr. Witherspoon!"

He reached for her hands and clasped them in his own,

his thumbs moving in a circular motion across the backs. His touch was not as comforting as Madison's had been, but neither was it unpleasant.

"Miss Hanssen, do forgive me if I am being too forward, but I have come to admire you a great deal and have developed a strong interest in you from the first day we met."

His eyes took on a softer look, but Elanna thought she detected a speck of fear, as well. She couldn't be sure, though.

"Our subsequent meetings only served to solidify that interest and make me certain of how I felt. With every question you posed and every smile you bestowed upon me when I was able to answer those queries, my affections have grown at an astounding rate."

She swallowed twice and moistened her dry lips. "I must say, Mr. Witherspoon, that this does come as a surprise to me to hear it stated so plainly."

He appeared hurt by her admission. "Surely, you must know that my interest in you is because of more than my business. I realize I did not state my intentions, but I thought you would know how I felt."

She nodded. "At times, I could see evidence of your interest, but as my heart had been previously resting in the hands of Major Scott, I was not free to return any affection."

"And now?"

Elanna inhaled and released the breath slowly. "Now, I am still uncertain. I feel I must wait until Major Scott has the opportunity to reply. Then I shall better know how I must proceed."

"But that could take months! By then, you could find out that you have wasted all this time, when you could marry me and begin a life full of adventure as we travel through the colonies and even venture across the ocean to England." He implored with his eyes. "Think of the exciting people we would see and the places we would go. Life would improve tenfold with you by my side."

She had to admit the life he presented to her sounded like a wonderful experience. She would get to see the world, learn fascinating facts, and maybe even meet Mama's family in England. But despite the allure, one truth remained clear.

"As appealing as that sounds, Mr. Witherspoon, I do not know if I am meant to travel the way that you do. I have lived my entire life here on my farm. And I enjoy it immensely. Should I begin a life of travel, I would miss my mama and papa and brothers and sister very much. Life here is exciting enough with the improvements being made by the assembly and the changes taking place. I know I can be happy right here."

"And you can have that, if you prefer," he assured her, once again resuming the circular motion of his thumbs. "I would be happy to leave you here while I travel on assignment if that is what you desire most. You will have everything your heart desires and every comfort you require. Then I would come home and share all of my stories with you."

He did an excellent job of presenting an appealing offer to her, but there were still too many holes she hadn't yet filled. Without every piece in place, she could not make a firm decision at this point.

"Mr. Witherspoon, I do appreciate your offer, and it is a most attractive one, to be certain." She withdrew her hands from his and placed them in her lap. "But I must decline for now. Upon receipt of Major Scott's response, I shall know better what must be done."

Defeat registered for a moment on his face, but a certain haughtiness also made itself known. It was as if he knew something she didn't, but he wasn't sharing it with her. If nothing else affirmed her decision, that did. Despite Mr.

Witherspoon's charm, she couldn't bring herself to turn her back on Madison just yet. Something told her to give him another chance, and she intended to do just that.

Standing, she extended one gloved hand in his direction. "Mr. Witherspoon, I promise to call again once I receive word from Major Scott."

He brushed a kiss across her knuckles and bowed ever so slightly. "Miss Hanssen, I shall await your return with great anticipation."

"Good day, Mr. Witherspoon," she said and left.

As she walked toward the carriage where her brother waited, she tried to decide if she should share any of this encounter with him. No, she needed to keep her mind clear of any outside influence. This decision was hers and hers alone. So for now, it would be between her and God—and Madison and Mr. Witherspoon, of course.

❧

Battle after battle had followed several smaller skirmishes for the duration of the winter months. On the heels of the British taking control of Fort Duquesne and cutting off the lines from Quebec and Ontario to the western forts, the French rallied in desperation. Madison and his men had been called to join other regiments in defense of their conquests. No sooner would they return from one battle, than they were engaging in the next.

In the midst of all of this, Madison had received another letter from Elanna. And although he hadn't had time to study it as thoroughly as he had all of her other letters, this one stood out in his mind. From the first words, his heart jumped into his throat. Her tone was softer and more personal, but he could still detect that same feeling of uncertainty between the lines she wrote. Her conclusion remained his favorite part:

Despite everything I have been told and the doubts that have entered my mind, I find myself returning to our brief time together before you were called away. We did not have much opportunity to share our hearts, but what we did share has remained imprinted on mine from the start. You have become quite special to me, and my thoughts are often centered on you as I go about my daily routine. I wonder what you might be doing at the very moment or if you think of me as often as I do you.

It is my sincerest wish that your reply will set everything right again. For in my heart of hearts, I cannot bring myself to betray you, no matter how solid the evidence is against you. Nevertheless, I do need your assurance and honesty regarding the matter at hand. If your response is as I imagine it will be, there will no longer be a need for uncertainty in my mind or in my heart. I am well aware of the struggles and challenges you face every day on the frontier, and I realize how easily that can affect a man's behavior or decisions in ways that are contrary to his very core. Despite this, however, I am confident you will provide an explanation for the reports that have filtered down to us.

My prayers are that I will not have to consider the alternative. Please write as soon as possible. I eagerly await your response.

Fondly yours,
Elanna

He had been enraged by the lies she had shared, courtesy of the journalist she had met. This Mr. Witherspoon had become a thorn in his side, and everything in him made Madison want to rush home to set the record straight. Her closing words had gone a long way toward tempering his anger, but every time he repeated in his mind those parts concerning Mr. Witherspoon's reports, the intense fury at the audacity of the journalist returned full force:

> *Mr. Witherspoon has shared with me, on two separate occasions, reports from his various sources that have painted you in a less than favorable light. Although I was hesitant to accept his word as truth, when he provided a documented report, what other choice did I have? It spoke of how you disobeyed orders and led your men in a brutal attack against the French and the Indians who had already surrendered. It also mentioned how you repeatedly put your men at risk with a disregard for their safety. I pray this is not true, but I must present this to you and ask for your response.*

Left with no other recourse than to turn his rage toward their enemy, Madison charged into the heart of the fighting. With his head otherwise occupied by Elanna's disturbing letter, he failed to realize that he had stumbled into an encampment where he was greatly outnumbered.

twelve

Madison tried to open his eyes, but the slightest pinprick of light sent shooting pain to his head. He moaned and sank farther into the feather tick, trying to figure out where he was. He wrinkled his nose when the foul stench of opiates hit his nostrils.

"Welcome back, Major. It is good to see you join us again."

He recognized Lewis's voice and tried again to open his eyes. This time, he managed to allow a sliver of light in without causing excruciating pain. With effort, he slowly worked at the task. First, he saw nothing but shadows; then a blurry image appeared. Blinking several times, his vision cleared enough for him to make out the concerned but happy face of Lieutenant Lewis. The walls seemed familiar, and he searched his memory for the answer.

The hospital! He was on the island across from Fort Edward. The fighting had all been farther north along Lake Champlain and Lake George. Some was as far as the Canadian border. How had he gotten back here?

"How. . . ," he rasped, his throat feeling like the bristles of the brush he used to comb his mount.

Lewis reached for the pitcher and poured water into a tin cup. With a hand behind Madison's head, Lewis helped him take a drink.

"How long have I been unconscious?" he tried again with more success.

"Nearly three days in addition to the two it took us to bring you back, sir," Lewis replied. "You took a nasty blow to the head and a muzzle to your back before we were able to come to your aid."

Madison shifted and gasped at the sharp pain that shot up his spine. A dull ache existed somewhere near the left side of his lower back. He figured that to be the bruise from the butt of the rifle. It felt like it spread clear across from side to side, and it hurt to move. With concerted effort, he raised his left arm and touched the bandaged spot on the side of his head. Thank God it didn't feel wet or sticky. His right arm was tucked across his chest in a sling-like fashion.

Everything was a blur to him. The last thing he remembered was charging into the French camp and encountering a larger force than he had reckoned. Elanna's face had flashed in his mind, and then all went black.

"Did . . ." He swallowed again to moisten his throat. "Did we gain another victory?"

Lewis nodded, and his chest puffed out with pride. "Once we saw what those French and Indians had done to you and had moved you to safety, we returned and gave them all we had, sir. They no doubt are still wondering what hit them."

Madison breathed a sigh of relief. He couldn't have been assigned a better regiment. His men stuck by him no matter what and were loyal to the end. Even if it meant risking their own lives, they would do it for anyone among their ranks.

"When I go into battle, Matthew, I would have no one else by my side," he stated, extending his left hand toward Lewis.

The lieutenant extended his own hand and the men clasped forearms, a more personal handshake they had learned from their Indian allies that intimated a stronger bond. As soon as Lewis let go, Madison let his arm fall back against the bed, worn out from the exertion.

"And I would have no one else lead me, sir."

"So where do we stand now?"

Lewis pulled a chair to the bedside and sat down. "The skirmishes have all but died down, and the French have pulled back their forces to concentrate them closer to the key strongholds of Quebec and Montreal."

His mind started to clear. "Does Major General Amherst still have plans to launch an attack on Quebec?"

"Actually, General James Wolfe is leading that attack. He arrived in Louisburg in early May and has started preparing his troops for their march inland. Other forces are leading an advance inland from Lake Champlain, and Admiral Saunders is commanding a fleet of forty-nine ships and 140 smaller craft to come to their aid."

"What is the word on when we will be called to join them?"

Lewis looked away for a moment and didn't offer an immediate answer. "I mean no disrespect, sir," he said and returned his gaze, full of regret, "but I have been told that your orders are to remain abed for at least another two weeks. They want to make certain you are fully recovered from your injuries and able to engage in battle again before you are sent out." His expression changed to one of admiration. "Your heroics have caused quite a stir over at the fort. It seems they value you too much to put you at great risk again so soon."

Hearing that gave Madison a feeling of gratification that his efforts hadn't gone unnoticed. But he didn't like being stuck in bed, unable to move about at will. He got restless if he didn't stay active. Already, after five days of being unconscious, he felt the effects of the stationary confinement.

"And what am I supposed to do for those two weeks while I wait for my body to recover to the general's satisfaction?"

"Oh, quit your moaning and take your penance like a man," Rogers said as he entered Madison's private room. He approached the bed and stood on the side opposite Lewis.

Dark stubble could be seen on his chin, and half of his hair had come loose from the pigtail. "I heard you had been brought here and invaded my territory."

Madison quirked an eyebrow, although he was sure Rogers couldn't see it from underneath the bandage. "*Your* territory? The last time I checked, this island belonged to the fort, and you are permitted to use it for the time being."

Rogers gave him a half-crooked grin. "All right, so I might have exaggerated a bit. But you are still over here where I train my rangers. I would say that is close enough."

He must have just left a recent training session and not taken the time to clean up before paying a visit. It only served to confirm the reasons he had yet to be promoted to anything more than a captain. With the precision the British used in their military strategies, they also required a certain appearance be maintained. Rogers fell far short of that mark, but no one could deny his prowess on the battlefield and ability to get the job done.

"So, what do you hear from commanding officers about this march on Quebec?" Madison directed his question toward Rogers.

"Probably less than Lewis, here," Rogers replied with a sweeping motion of his arm across the bed. "I have been too busy here on the island, getting my rangers ready for battle, to pay attention to any strategic planning taking place inside the fort."

"Well, I know I count on you both"—Madison included the two of them in his gaze—"to inform me of any developments and the latest information as soon as you learn of it."

Both men saluted, but Madison caught a twinkle in their eyes, too.

"Aye, aye, Major," Rogers replied in a gravelly voice as he thumped his fist across his chest. Lewis mirrored the action.

"We live to serve and swear our eternal allegiance to your command."

Madison started to laugh at their antics, but the effort aggravated the pain in his back and sides, so he resorted to a soft chuckle that didn't hurt as much. "How a man ever accomplishes anything with jesters such as yourselves under his command is beyond me," he retorted.

Lewis grew serious. "When faced with the atrocities of this war, what other recourse do we have?"

Madison formed his lips into a grim line. "With as much death and destruction as we have seen, it is a wonder that any of us are still able to find any lightheartedness."

"When we no longer can," Rogers replied, "we will know the end is near."

That was a solemn and morose remark if Madison ever heard one. Thoughts like that would serve no purpose for them now.

"All right. I believe I should take time to rest, and you two should be about your business. I have my health to regain if I am to be ready to join the regiments headed north to Quebec in a couple of weeks."

Rogers looked across the bed at Lewis. "I believe that was a dismissal."

Lewis nodded. "I believe you are right." He stood, and Rogers joined him. "Shall we?"

Before they left, Rogers looked over his shoulder at Madison.

"You send for me if you need anything. I might come; I might not." He grinned. "But I will be here if I can."

"The same goes for me," Lewis echoed.

Madison offered a weak salute. "Thank you to you both."

With reciprocating salutes, they were gone, and Madison was left alone with only his thoughts to keep him company.

Once again, he found himself replaying the contents of

Elanna's letter in his mind. At that, he turned his head to the left and right and looked for any sign of his journal. If he was going to be in bed for two weeks, he intended to make good use of that time and write the letter to Elanna that he had been wanting to write for over a year.

Not seeing the journal anywhere, Madison started to rise but fell back against the bed, breathing heavily to ward off the pain.

"Is there something you need, sir?"

He glanced toward the door to the hallway to see a young lad holding a tray. As he approached, Madison saw the trencher with a pale-colored broth inside. Despite the decided lack of meat in what he assumed was supposed to be stew, the aroma made his stomach growl.

The lad laughed. "I wish it was something more substantial, but you have to start off with small portions to make sure you can keep everything down. Your stomach will no doubt be grateful for the nourishment."

After helping him to a partial sitting position, the lad deposited the tray and started to leave Madison alone to eat. When he was halfway to the door, he stopped.

"Were you looking for something in particular, sir? Something else I can get for you?"

Madison swallowed, then lowered the spoon from his mouth. "My journal. It would have been among my personal things when I was brought here."

Recognition dawned on the lad's face. "Ah, yes. It was put in this box for safe keeping." He walked to the table and lifted the lid on what appeared to be an apothecary box. From inside, he withdrew Madison's journal and brought it to the table next to the bed. "Here you are, sir. Will there be anything else?"

"No, thank you."

The lad headed once more for the door. "I will come back

for the trencher when you are done."

Making short order of the first meal he'd had in days, Madison set the tray aside and reached for his journal. Relieved that the pencil remained tucked inside, he pulled out several sheets of paper and began.

9 July 1759
My dearest Elanna,

  Thank you for your honesty in the most recent letter you sent. I could ascertain how difficult it was for you to put to me such bold and direct questions, but it is good that we have everything out in the open. As I stated previously, I had been rather confused by the change in your tone and emotion from previous correspondence. Now that I am aware of the source, I am better prepared to send you an explanation.

  The mere idea that Mr. Witherspoon would have received reports of my disobedience or lack of regard for safety for my men has caused a great deal of anger on my part. I do not know what his supposed sources are, but I can assure you that they cannot be further from the truth. I realize that without me there in front of you, presenting proof to refute the lies he has concocted, you must rely solely on the opinions you have formed about me. But it is my sincerest prayer that you would look deep into your heart and know that I am not guilty of such heinous acts. Although the thoughts did enter my mind to return equal brutality on the French and the Indians, my men and the knowledge that our good Lord would not approve kept me from acting on those thoughts.

He thanked God again for keeping him from committing acts that might have caused disastrous results. Despite the rage that surged within him following some of the savage attacks, he had been able to temper it with enough assurance that the French would receive their just punishment. Had he not, the reports Mr. Witherspoon had fabricated might have very well been true.

I do not know anything about this journalist, other than what you have told me, but the fact that he would falsify something to that great extent makes me wish I was there with you to protect you from whatever schemes he might have. Should he also have it in his mind to lure you away for his own benefit, I pray you exercise great caution when you are alone with him.

And now, I have a confession to make. Throughout the entire winter, our armies were engaged in a series of battles and skirmishes that kept us occupied for several months. Your letter arrived amidst the flurry of activity, and I had precious little time to peruse it before being called back to fight. When I was finally able to read to the end and learned of the duplicitous nature of Mr. Witherspoon, a fierce anger burned inside of me.

He didn't want to cause her any great concern, so he made sure to lessen the intensity of his feelings. If he was going to prove to her that he would never do what Witherspoon accused him of doing, he had to tread lightly.

Because I was unable to rush home to you and defend my honor, I channeled that anger toward the only source I had at my disposal. Fighting against the French with renewed vigor, we saw victory after victory come from our efforts. With your words burned in my mind, and in an act of appalling judgment, I charged into a camp without scouting it out first. The regiment we faced outnumbered my own.

As a result, my injuries have put me in the infirmary with orders to remain here for at least two weeks while the armies mount a major attack.

I do not know what the outcome will be, so I wanted to write this letter to you now. Should the results prove to be in our favor, I will come back and add a small note to the end, sharing the good news. Until that time, know that I eagerly await the opportunity to leave this barren frontier and return to New Castle where I pray you will be waiting for me with open arms. I can assure you that my intentions where you are concerned are honorable and, should you return my affections, of a permanent nature.

Madison paused, wondering if he should be so bold. Then again, why not? At a time when Elanna doubted his sincerity or even his honor, he had to make it clear to her where he stood. He had to convey to her that he wanted her for his wife and he would do whatever was necessary to make that happen.

Thoughts of you keep me going day by day, but they are nothing compared to the reality of being with you where I can show you how I feel. And once that happens, I desire to never again be apart from you. I have even entertained the notion of moving to a new home and getting involved with the shipbuilding industry in Wilmington. My skill with iron would come in handy in that trade.

Please give all that I offer careful consideration. I pray that our next communication will be face-to-face. Until then, my heart is in your hands.

With fond affection,
Forever yours,
Madison

He prayed the postscript he mentioned would become a reality and he could make plans to return to Elanna.

❧

Madison slipped behind the cover of trees not too far from the road to Sillery. His regiment had all found hiding places as well, and he drew his closest leaders to his side.

"General Wolfe has landed near Anse-aux-Foulons Cove, three kilometers upstream from Quebec. The British Navy has blockaded the ports in France, and the minor attacks along the St. Lawrence River have reduced the provisions the French have at hand. We are poised at the perfect opportunity to attack."

"Major, what about Captain Vergor?" Sergeant Davis asked.

"Wolfe's men have taken Vergor's camp and established a solid foothold at the top of the cliffs," Madison replied. "We have no need to concern ourselves with him."

"What are our orders?" This came from Captain Randolph.

"We are to join Wolfe's army on the right flank, with our backs to the water. We will be anchored by the bluffs along the St. Lawrence as the line will spread out across the plains and enter into a horseshoe formation."

"I say we are ready!" Lewis exclaimed. "Let us not delay further."

Madison thrilled at the excitement surrounding this attack. With the progress they'd made thus far, he could taste their victory close at hand. All they had to do was push through the French lines into Quebec.

"Men!" Madison commanded. "Let us march!"

In a matter of hours, they had joined Brigadier-General Townshend's regiment and exchanged fire with the French militia hiding in the scrub. In retaliation to the British capturing a small collection of houses and gristmill to anchor their line, the French lit several houses on fire to keep them out of the hands of the British. Smoke from the fires masked the British left flank. Madison looked across the plains and down the line. The steady fire nearly concealed Wolfe's men from view. Before long, he heard the order from Wolfe for his men to lie down amid the high grass and brush.

As the French advanced, commands echoed throughout the regiments.

"Hold the line!"

"Hold your fire!"

If Madison had not been instructed beforehand, he might have stumbled at such orders. It seemed counterproductive to hold fire while the enemy attacked, but when the French were within twenty paces, the British opened fire at close range. The startled faces of the French were enough to bolster Madison's men and strengthen their resolve as they advanced for the second round of fire that sent the French in retreat.

All of a sudden, everything changed. Word reached Madison that Wolfe had fallen after he led a small contingent to a rise above the battle. With several other officers wounded, their line fell into disorganized chaos as they chased the retreating French toward Quebec. There, the British were met with heavy fire by the French from the direction of the bridge over the St. Charles.

Madison caught sight of Randolph, Lewis, and Davis, who all looked to him for new orders. In a panic, Madison searched for Townshend and saw him rally the troops. The general quickly formed up two battalions from the confused troops on the field and turned them to meet the oncoming French at the rear who had gathered reinforcements and were mounting a counterattack. Madison led his men to follow suit as they fought with bayonets and swords to keep the French from breaking through their lines. Colonel Bougainville retreated while the rest of Montcalm's army slipped back across the St. Charles.

Over the next few days, after Montcalm suffered a mortal wound to the leg and abdomen, a state of confusion spread through the French troops. Madison had never seen such disorder and turmoil among soldiers. Even when the British and colonists had lost Wolfe, Townshend quickly took charge. The commander who replaced Vaudreuil for the French, however, abandoned Quebec and the Beauport shore, ordering all of his forces to march west. Madison led his regiment with the rest of the British troops as they besieged the city and received additional support from Admiral Saunders's fleet.

With careful petitioning, Madison had the opportunity to be present on the eighteenth of September, when de Ramezay, Townshend, and Saunders signed a treaty that turned the city of Quebec over to British control. He returned to his men sequestered in town and watched their celebration, toasting with port and a selection of fine wines, courtesy of the French. He had never been one for imbibing, so despite the strong appeal due to the circumstances, he refrained.

Later that night, he settled into the feathery softness of his bed and pulled out his journal again. He almost couldn't contain his joy at being able to finish his letter to Elanna and tell her the good news. After scratching out his previous closing signature, he added a little more:

As promised, my dear, I am adding a few extra words to share of the victory we have received this day. After nearly four months, we have control of one of the great cities in the north and have blown several gaping holes in the French defense. It will take them months to recover. I know it is just five weeks past your eighteenth birthday, and while I had hoped to have returned by then, I can promise you now a return before winter arrives.

I will be with you again before Christmas, and I pray my reception will be one of anticipation equal to the joy I feel in my heart, knowing I will soon see your beautiful face. There is so much to say and so much I want to hear from you, but I will wait until we are together.

All my love,
Madison

As he drifted off to sleep, he tried to center his thoughts on a joyous reunion with Elanna. But he couldn't prevent the doubt that shadowed his dreams. Just what kind of reception would he find in New Castle?

thirteen

"That is the last one!" Mama called from above after handing Elanna a jar of peach preserves.

Elanna climbed up the ladder from the root cellar. "Are you certain there are no more jars hiding in the corners?" she teased with a grin as she lowered the door and locked the latch. Walking toward the fireplace, she extended her hands to warm them. For not being very far below ground, the cellar stayed quite cold.

Mama pushed a fist against the small of her back, then poured cider for herself and Elanna. "I do not understand it. Each year, the number of jars seems to grow."

"That is because our farm is growing and we have more mouths to feed."

"That is quite true." Mama nodded, regarding Elanna over the rim of her cup with a twinkle in her eyes. "What news do you hear from Major Scott?"

Heat rushed to her cheeks as Elanna recalled the words Madison had written in his last letter. She couldn't share the details of that with Mama, so she searched her mind for what she *could* repeat.

"He is well," she replied, "although he did spend several weeks earlier this year at the infirmary, recovering from minor injuries he sustained during one of the skirmishes."

"I am amazed that he has avoided more serious wounds, considering how long he has been fighting and the dangers he faces."

Elanna had been thankful to God for that very thing. "Our

Lord above must surely be going with him into every battle, Mama. God has kept him safe from the grip of death and helped keep him strong despite the oppressive circumstances."

Mama gave her a knowing look. "And what of the dilemma you faced not long ago?"

Inner turmoil once again surfaced, and a feeling of melancholy washed over Elanna. She sighed. "I am no closer to a solution now than I was three months ago, Mama." She wrung her hands on her apron and paced in front of the fireplace. "Mad—Major Scott," she corrected herself, "has assured me that the reports Mr. Witherspoon presented were in some way falsified. Mr. Witherspoon assures me they are not. He is here, and Madison is not." She halted and looked at Mama. "Who am I to believe?"

Mama pursed her lips, empathy shining in her eyes. "My daughter, I would love more than anything to solve this problem for you, but I cannot. It is not an easy decision, and someone will be hurt regardless of what you decide." Mama approached to stand in front of Elanna and touch her cheek. "But you are eighteen now, and this is something you must solve on your own. Trust God, Elanna. He will guide you through the darkest hour. Surrender your troubles to Him, and He will direct you down the path you must take."

Tears gathered in Elanna's eyes at Mama's words. Throwing her arms around her mother, she shared a tight embrace, then pulled back and placed a kiss on Mama's cheek.

"Thank you," she whispered, unable to find her voice beyond the lump in her throat.

"Be strengthened, child," Mama replied and gave Elanna a nudge toward the hall. "Now, be off with you. I believe you and God have a conversation that is long overdue."

Elanna located her wrap and headed outside to her favorite spot beneath the trees in the grove to the west. The chill of late autumn and the last remaining leaves of color told of the impending winter. Harvest was her favorite time of year, second only to Christmas. She enjoyed the spring as well, with its newness of life, but something about the celebration of the harvest and rejoicing in another completed season filled her like nothing else. Christmas only made this time even better.

As she reached her favorite spot, her confusion over Madison and Mr. Witherspoon once again took precedence in her thoughts. Mama had told her to seek the Lord's will and He would guide her. It seemed so simple yet felt so difficult. She thought she had been asking God all along, but if she truly had, would she be in this predicament now?

After all, what did she know about Mr. Witherspoon, other than his obvious social standing and notoriety as a sought-after journalist? Yes, he had impeccable manners, and he had always appeared to put her interests first whenever they were together. But what had he shared about his personal life?

Madison, on the other hand, had told her everything in his letters. He spoke of Boston, his family, his years as a child and young man, his fears and plans for the future. And added to that was his consideration of moving to Wilmington to be closer to her. Mr. Witherspoon was already in Wilmington, but would she be happy as the wife of a journalist who spent more time away than at home?

So much about the decision seemed clear, but a part of her still labored over the two choices. Both men presented her with options that appealed to her in different ways. Each one had his own merits. But without Madison here in front of her, she simply couldn't make up her mind. She needed him here, so she could look him in the eyes and know for sure. His eyes would never lie.

Two whinnies from the corral adjacent to the grove caught

her attention. Valdig, Mama's horse, did a little sidestep as he nodded his head up and down, as if he agreed with her. Elanna giggled and walked toward the fence. Valdig met her there and stretched his head over the fence to nuzzle her cheek. She scratched the horse's forelock, then patted his jowls. In response, Valdig started nudging her arm, looking for a treat. He might be old, but he was still ornery.

She laughed and held out her hands. "I am sorry, boy, but I have nothing with me this time."

A sharp whistle from the barn followed her words, and Valdig perked his ears at the sound. The horse looked over his shoulder and lumbered in that direction. His steps faltered a bit, but he managed to recover.

"Traitor!" Elanna called to Valdig's retreating back. As she watched him disappear inside the barn, she wondered if God had sent the horse to her for a reason. Propping her arms on the top rail of the fence, she closed her eyes and started to pray.

"Most gracious Father above, Thou art sovereign above all else. Thy kingdom reigns over everyone, and Thy favor rests on those who serve Thee. I know Thou hast planned a path for me, but I am unable to see it through the clouded vision of my confusion. I ask that Thou wilt show me clearly the way I am to walk. Present to me the truth so that I will no longer be led astray by the wrong choice. I trust in Thy divine wisdom, both now and always. Thank Thee, Father, for hearing my cry. Amen."

Relief upon closing her prayer washed over her. She still didn't have an answer, but she felt confident that God would bring it to her soon.

"Elanna!"

She looked toward the house, where her brother Jerel waved from the front step.

"You have a caller!"

Madison! Her heart leaped in her chest. Could it be he? Had the answer to her prayer truly come this quickly? There was only one way to find out. Lifting her petticoats with one hand and tucking the wrap close to her neck with the other, Elanna set off at a brisk pace, eager to see who had come to call.

She paused before entering to regain her breath, set her petticoats to right again, and check her coiffed hair. A chill traveled up her spine at the thought of who might be waiting for her. With another deep breath, she pushed open the door and stepped inside. After removing her wrap and handing it to the servant girl waiting for her, Elanna took the few steps toward the parlor. At the sound of her presence, Mr. Witherspoon stood with a welcome smile on his face.

Elanna closed her eyes and tried to hide her disappointment. "Mr. Witherspoon," she greeted as she stepped into the room and forced a smile to her lips.

He clasped her hands in his, the warmth seeping through her gloves. "Miss Hanssen, do forgive me for this unannounced visit, but I could not wait any longer."

Bewilderment made her tilt her head and draw her eyebrows together. "I am afraid you have me at a distinct disadvantage, Mr. Witherspoon. Is there something so pressing that you could not have sent for me to meet you at your office?"

"Yes," he replied without hesitation. "I believe I have been most patient regarding our relationship, Miss Hanssen, and I have permitted your fanciful notions while you waited for a letter from Major Scott."

Fanciful notions? Elanna didn't like where this was headed. If he had come to ask for her hand, he had better be more careful in the words he chose.

He led her to the settee and silently encouraged her to sit. With her hands still caught in his, she had no other choice than to listen to what he had to say.

"Now that you have attained your eighteenth year, it is time for you to make a decision about your future. I have not yet spoken with your father, as I would like to hear the words from your lips first."

Oh please, not now, Elanna prayed. Could this be the answer she had asked God to provide? She had heard of Him responding immediately in some situations, but couldn't He wait just a little longer? She still wasn't sure she was ready to make a decision.

Mr. Witherspoon continued as if the war that was taking place in her heart and mind didn't exist.

"Miss Hanssen, I have come to care quite deeply for you, and I vow to cherish you better than any man would. Your wishes and desires will always be put ahead of my own, and I pledge to provide for your every need." The earnestness in his eyes held her gaze. "Now, will you do me the honor of—"

"Elanna!"

Mr. Witherspoon started and immediately dropped her hands at the intrusion.

Edric nearly stumbled into the parlor. "You will never guess who Father and I met along the way home from town."

He looked near to bursting with what appeared to be big news. Mr. Witherspoon coughed and cleared his throat. Edric gave him a look that resembled more of a glare than a courteous acknowledgment of a guest in their home.

"Well, are you going to tell me, or will I remain in suspense?" Elanna asked, bringing Edric's attention back to her.

"Perhaps it would be better if I announced myself," a familiar voice said from behind Edric.

Elanna gasped as Thomas McKean appeared in the

doorway, followed by Papa, who also frowned when he saw Mr. Witherspoon standing next to her. What exactly was wrong with Papa and Edric? And what purpose would the esteemed councilman have in coming to their home when a meeting of the assembly was not taking place?

Mr. McKean approached and raised her hand to his lips. "Miss Hanssen, your brother and father have told me a lot about you," he said with a twinkle in his eye. "Our carriages happened to pass on the road between here and town. Although assembly matters occupied the majority of our conversation, another matter soon became of great importance." When he glanced to the side and looked at Mr. Witherspoon, his lips formed a straight line.

She felt more than saw the journalist shrink under Mr. McKean's penetrating stare. Edric, Papa, and Mr. McKean didn't seem to hold Mr. Witherspoon in high regard. Before she could give voice to the question poised on her lips, Edric stepped forward. Behind him, and standing next to Papa in the hall, were Jerel and Kare.

"Elanna, I know you made me promise not to share too much about your correspondence with Major Scott—and I haven't," Edric rushed to add. "But I also know you have not been happy of late. More often than not, I see you with a frown on your face rather than the smiles you had when you were first writing to the major." He looked over his shoulder at Papa, who nodded, and Edric continued, but not without another glare at Mr. Witherspoon. "When you showed me that report about Major Scott during the attack on Fort Frontenac up north, something about it did not set right with me. Until I had the opportunity to speak to Mr. McKean, my mind was in a constant state of unrest." He sent an appreciative smile in the councilmen's direction. "But that is not the case any longer."

A sinking feeling settled in Elanna's stomach. With the way the men were all looking at Mr. Witherspoon, this news could not be good. The journalist didn't appear affected, though. He seemed undaunted and at ease. But without being fully informed of the matter at hand, she could offer neither defense nor sentence.

Mr. McKean stepped back so he could address everyone present. Papa, Jerel, and Kare came fully into the parlor. With the somber expressions on all of their faces, Elanna felt more like a child about to be scolded than a young woman with an unknown truth about to be revealed.

"Miss Hanssen, it has come to my attention that certain reports have been presented to you regarding a fellow colonist fighting with the British army in the war up north. As deputy attorney general in Sussex County, I am privy to much information that is not available to most."

She nodded, praying he would get to the point.

"Would you be so kind as to bring the report to me, so that I might see it for myself?"

"Of course," Elanna replied and rushed upstairs to retrieve the paper Mr. Witherspoon had given her.

When she returned and passed the page to Mr. McKean, silence fell upon everyone in the room as the councilman perused what had been written. After what felt like an eternity, McKean finally spoke.

"I regret to inform you," he began with a withering glare directed at Mr. Witherspoon, "that this report and the others were falsified. The truth of them has been greatly exaggerated."

Her breath caught in her throat, and she covered her mouth to hide the gasp that followed. Falsified reports? But why? The councilman had not withdrawn his gaze from the journalist, and she could hear Witherspoon swallow several times as he cowered behind her. She resisted the urge to look over her shoulder at him and tried hard to control the anger that burned inside at this revelation.

"It appears that Mr. Witherspoon tampered with the veracity of the reports he received from several couriers and replaced the names of other soldiers and officers with that of Major Scott." He cleared his throat. "Now, I do not abide deception in any form, but especially not from someone with a position of such high esteem in this county."

Unable to resist any longer, Elanna turned to look at Mr. Witherspoon. His face had paled considerably, and beads of sweat appeared on his forehead.

"How could you?" she seethed.

The journalist looked down at her and shifted from one foot to the other as he kept watch on her brothers, Papa, and Mr. McKean from the corner of his eye.

"I—I," he stammered. "I did it because I did not want to see you make a mistake with a man who might never return."

The excuse fell flat, and from the defeated look on Mr. Witherspoon's face, it seemed he knew it.

Elanna stood and faced him, praying for patience. "The only mistake I have made is allowing you to lead me astray with your lies. I cannot believe your charming nature has fooled me to the point that I actually considered accepting your proposal."

A spark flashed in his eyes at her words but dimmed when he again caught sight of the other men in the room. "Please forgive me, Miss Hanssen. I confess to my wrongdoing, but I cannot leave without knowing that despite your feelings of betrayal, you can find it in your heart to offer forgiveness."

Although every fiber inside of her screamed to deny him his request, a still, small voice told her she should forgive him. He would receive his just penalty for his actions. It was not up to her to levy judgment on him.

With sadness in her heart, she held his eyes. "I do forgive you, Mr. Witherspoon, and I pray that you will learn from your mistakes, not repeat them."

He nodded but didn't reply.

Papa stepped forward, his jaw clenched and his fists tightened at his sides. "I believe it is time for you to leave, Mr. Witherspoon," he said with a menacing tone. "Otherwise, your punishment might be delivered here instead of by the assembly in town."

Mr. McKean remained tight-lipped, but mirth danced in his eyes. "I believe time spent at the pillory or a few dips on the ducking stool would suffice."

Elanna held back the reflexive chuckle at the councilman's jesting. As promising as that punishment might be, Mr. Witherspoon would no doubt receive only a fine due to his family's social standing.

Not needing further encouragement and looking as if he didn't know whether or not Mr. McKean was serious, the journalist almost ran from the house. A minute later, she heard his horse galloping away, and relief washed over her. She silently sent thanks to God for His immediate answer to her prayer and for the love and protection of her family that kept her from making the biggest mistake of her life.

After a round of hugs, and a smile of thanks to Mr. McKean, Elanna started to leave the men, but Papa blocked her path.

"I suppose now I should give you this," he said with a smile and handed an envelope to her.

Elanna glanced down at it and inhaled. The familiar handwriting addressing the letter to her brought an even bigger smile to her lips. Unable to contain her excitement, she tore open the letter and read the short missive inside:

15 November 1759
My Dearest Elanna,

   By the time you receive this letter, I will be near New
Castle. Our efforts in the war have met with great success.
And although the fighting continues, I have been granted
permission to take my leave for a brief period in order
that I might come for a visit. I am writing this from
Philadelphia where I am meeting with several councilmen
on official business for the army. If there are no unforeseen
delays, I should arrive Wednesday next. I can only pray that
my reception will be as warm as are my thoughts of you.
Longing to see you face-to-face again, I remain:

Forever yours,
Madison

Moisture gathered in Elanna's eyes at his words. She bit
her lower lip as she looked at Papa, his smile blurry through
her tears.

"I trust the news is good?"

She turned to Mr. McKean, who wore an amused expression.

"Major Sco—" She swallowed beyond the catch in her
throat and tried again. "Major Scott is coming home!"

&

Elanna tried for the hundredth time to calm her rapidly
beating heart or gain control of her breathing, all to no avail.
Wednesday had arrived. A light dusting of snow had fallen
overnight, and she pulled her cloak tighter around her to
ward off the chill in the air. At any moment, Madison would
appear at the end of the tree-lined lane leading to the road.
Over three years had passed. Would he look the same as she
remembered?

A horse and rider came into sight. Madison! Her heart
leaped with joy. This time, she knew the identity of the person

coming to call. Her legs trembled, and several shivers traveled up her back as he drew closer. At first, she wondered why he ambled so slowly. He should be galloping at full speed in her direction. Then she remembered. Not knowing the status of her heart, he wouldn't presume. Waiting was pure torture. The lane never seemed so long.

Finally, unable to contain her excitement, she grabbed two handfuls of her petticoats and took off at a full run toward Madison. He drew up his horse and hesitated, as if trying to decide what to do. As she drew near, all hesitation vanished. He leaped from the saddle and closed the distance between them with just a few steps, catching hold of her in his strong arms and swinging her around.

"Elanna," he breathed into her ear, then slowly lowered her to the ground. "I can scarce believe my eyes. I have dreamed of this moment for what seems like an eternity. Now, here you stand before me." He peered down at her, the intensity in his gaze nearly overwhelming. "And with love shining in your eyes!"

"Oh, Madison," she whispered, unable to speak as tears pooled and slid down her cheeks.

He tenderly brushed them away, then touched his finger to his lips. His eyes darkened as his gaze fell to her mouth.

"I suppose the answer is quite obvious, but for the sake of propriety, I must ask." He flicked his gaze up to meet hers. "Miss Elanna Hanssen, will you do me the honor of becoming my wife?"

She jumped into his arms again and squealed. "Yes! Yes! A thousand times, yes!"

Laughter rumbled in his chest as he hugged her to him. He pulled back just enough for her to see the sparkle in his eyes. The joy seemed to spring up from his soul. His expression softened as he studied her lips. Elanna smiled, inviting his touch. Locking her arms more tightly around his neck, she sealed their vow with the unconditional acceptance of their two lives now joined as one.

epilogue

Madison paced back and forth in the narrow hallway outside their bedchamber. The cries of his wife nearly undid him. If it hadn't been for the reassuring presence of his father-in-law, Gustaf Hanssen, he might have passed out from the anxiety. How Mr. Hanssen had endured this five times over was beyond him. Madison didn't think he'd make it through the first.

Finally, a slap followed by the robust cry of an infant sounded from behind the closed door. Madison expelled the breath he'd been holding and nearly collapsed in relief. He stared at the door, waiting for the pronouncement.

Please, let Elanna and our child be all right, he prayed silently.

Just as he opened his eyes, the door opened, and the midwife stepped out. He searched her face for any sign of concern or distress. When her eyes met his, she smiled.

"Mr. Scott, you and your wife have a healthy baby girl."

A girl! Elanna and he had a girl.

"My wife?"

The midwife placed a hand on his shoulder. "She is well. A bit tired, but that is to be expected." She stepped aside. "You may go in, now, but be sure to not overtax your wife."

Madison nodded and brushed past the woman, heading straight for Elanna's side. Raelene Hanssen stood off to the side, washing her hands in the basin on the stand.

Elanna turned to him and beamed a smile. "We have a girl, Madison."

He lifted her hand to his lips and pressed a kiss to her knuckles, then flattened her palm against his cheek. "Yes, my love, I know."

She freed her hand from his to pull back the swaddling from their daughter's face. A pink cherub with tiny slits for eyes peeked out from the blankets. She seemed so content in Elanna's arms. A strong feeling of love washed over him as he beheld the life they had created. His wife leaned back a little and peered around him, smiling again.

"Papa, come meet your granddaughter, Margret."

Gustaf Hanssen joined his wife on the other side of the bed and put his arm around her waist as the two gazed down at little Margret. Madison reached out to touch his daughter's smooth skin, and she stirred.

"I believe she likes you," Elanna teased. "She recognizes her papa."

"I cannot express how happy I am at this moment," he began. "All of North America is in the hands of the British, we have successfully sent the French back across the ocean, I have begun my trade in the shipbuilding industry, and I have a brand-new daughter to celebrate the love I share with my wife." He brushed the damp hair away from Elanna's forehead and leaned down to place a kiss there. "Life cannot get any better than this."

"Amen to that," Elanna answered softly.

As Madison beheld the beautiful face of his newborn daughter, he prayed that she would never be separated from her loved ones the way the war had kept him from Elanna. But as his experience had proven, change could come at any moment. Wars, accidents, crop failures, death. They could all strike without warning. Still, Madison knew that wherever life took them, God's protection would always be close at hand.

He pulled up a stool and sat before his wife and daughter. God had brought them this far. And He'd be there until the end, no matter what happened.

author's note

You no doubt noticed that there are many references to actual historical details, including names, dates, locations, and events, scattered throughout this book. While all of those are true and factual, the conversations that take place between the characters and the dialogue spoken by actual historical figures are all fictional. They are the result of a combination from a variety of sources and research, but those words were never documented as being spoken by those people. All other details and facts about those people, or those events, are real.

Other items such as the *New York Mercury*, *Pennsylvania Gazette*, and *Maryland Gazette* are actual newspapers that were in circulation at the time in which this book is set. However, the *Wilmington Journal* did not exist until 1785 as the *Delaware Gazette*. Various print editions to communicate the news were put out by smaller print shops in New Castle, Wilmington, and Dover, but no organized newspaper existed.

A Letter To Our Readers

Dear Reader:

In order that we might better contribute to your reading enjoyment, we would appreciate your taking a few minutes to respond to the following questions. We welcome your comments and read each form and letter we receive. When completed, please return to the following:

Fiction Editor
Heartsong Presents
PO Box 719
Uhrichsville, Ohio 44683

. Did you enjoy reading *Quills and Promises* by Amber Miller?
   ❑ Very much! I would like to see more books by this author!
   ❑ Moderately. I would have enjoyed it more if

   _____

   _____

   _____

. Are you a member of **Heartsong Presents**? ❑ Yes ❑ No
   If no, where did you purchase this book? _____

   _____

. How would you rate, on a scale from 1 (poor) to 5 (superior), the cover design? _____

. On a scale from 1 (poor) to 10 (superior), please rate the following elements.

   _____ Heroine   _____ Plot
   _____ Hero   _____ Inspirational theme
   _____ Setting   _____ Secondary characters

5. These characters were special because? _____

_____

_____

6. How has this book inspired your life? _____

_____

_____

7. What settings would you like to see covered in future
   Heartsong Presents books? _____

_____

_____

8. What are some inspirational themes you would like to see
   treated in future books? _____

_____

_____

9. Would you be interested in reading other **Heartsong
   Presents** titles? ❏ Yes ❏ No

10. Please check your age range:
    ❏ Under 18   ❏ 18-24
    ❏ 25-34   ❏ 35-45
    ❏ 46-55   ❏ Over 55

Name _____

Occupation _____

Address _____

City, State, Zip _____

VIRGINIA BRIDES

3 stories in 1

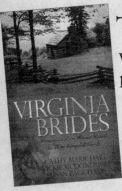

Traverse through Shenandoah Valley history. . .and love. When love starts to grow, will life's complications be too much to overcome? Can God bring good out of lives that seem to be spinning out of control?

Historical, paperback, 352 pages, 5³⁄₁₆" x 8"

_____